KINGSTON

SAVAGE DRAGONS BOOK 2

KATHI S. BARTON

This is a work of fiction. Names, characters, places, and incidents are products of the author's imagination or are used fictitiously and are not to be construed as real. Any resemblance to actual events, locations, organizations, or persons, living or dead, is entirely coincidental.

World Castle Publishing, LLC
Pensacola, Florida
Copyright © 2025 Kathi S. Barton
Hardback ISBN: 9798297847514
Paperback ISBN: 9798891264557
eBook ISBN: 9798891264564
First Edition World Castle Publishing, LLC, August 18, 2025
http://www.worldcastlepublishing.com
Licensing Notes
Cover: Cover Designs by Karen
Editor: Karen Fuller

Prologue

Kaida walked up and down the street a third time. Something or someone was calling for her, and she didn't understand the freaking magic that was having her walking the street like some kind of idiot. As she passed the restaurant once more, she decided that she was going to eat. Maybe that was all it was. She needed some food, and the magic was telling her to get her ass in gear and eat.

"You couldn't just say that, could you?" Waiting to be seated, she felt this was right. The place was calling to her, and she was going to sit down and have a good meal. As she was being seated, Kaida bumped ever so slightly into the waitress who was coming toward her and nearly fell to the ground when the surge of power washed over her. Sitting down rather than chancing another step, the woman asked her if she was all right. Simply putting her hand onto her arm told her everything she needed to know about the other woman.

"He's coming for you. Today. You're not safe here." The girl looked around before jerking her arm from her. "He's your ex-husband, and he wants your son. I can protect you."

"What are you talking about?" She laughed, but it was strained. "I don't have any children, nor have I ever been married." Pulling her hand to her, she pointed to the marks where a band might have been.

His name is Jason, and your name is Skye. Your last name is Houston, but you changed it to Wilson so that you could find a job. The people here think that your first name is Amanda. Your son's name is Matt. He's ten. Very smart for his age because you've been tutoring him for the last four years." She put her hand on her arm again. "Your parents are both dead, and you believe that Jason killed them. Your son is right now hiding out in an abandoned home so that he can be safe."

"What are you talking about?" Skye looked around before standing up. "Lady, I don't know where you got your information, but you're wrong. About it all."

"He'll be coming through the door with a gun in about two minutes." Instead of arguing with her more, she took off her apron and headed to the back of the place. Kaida told her to come and sit with her. He'd never see her if she did. "I promise you, Skye, he'll never touch either of you again."

Instead of arguing anymore, she slipped into the empty booth next to them, and Kaida joined her. Almost as soon as she put her arm around her shoulder, the door opened, and just as she said, a man came in with a gun pointed at the place. The small whimper that Skye made had nearly had her jump out of her skin when the man looked in their direction.

Shooting his gun to the ceiling, he asked where she was. He was looking for Skye Houston, and they had better turn her over to him, or he'll kill someone every ten minutes if they don't bring her to him.

"I don't know any Skye Houston." The manager looked around and then back to the man. "I have staff here by the name of Amanda and Carol Anne. Other than that, I can't help you."

Jason pointed the gun at the man's head, and it was all she could do not to get up and slam her magic into the man and kill him. Instead, she reached out to all the family and begged them to come to her. That she had a problem she was in over her head with. It was Tucker who answered her first and asked her where she was.

After telling them all what was going on she also told them that she was hiding a woman by the name of Skye. Also, that someone needed to go and get her son, or he might well be in trouble as well. It was Kings that said he'd get the boy, at least make sure that he was all right.

She knew that Skye's son would be all right with Kings watching over him, and she was never so happy with anyone as she was to see Tucker and Brenin come into the place next. With a short pop to the back of the head, the man was down, and his gun went flying.

For the silence when the man fell to the floor, there was so much noise that she wanted to clamp her hand over Skye's mouth to shut her up. Instead, all she did was put her hands over hers and tell her to calm down.

"I have to go to Matt." She told her that he was fine. The look she gave her had Kaida thinking that she didn't believe her. "He's all I have in the world. We've been running for the last five years, and I need to keep him safe."

"I understand that. But he's with my cousin-in-law, and he's bringing him here to you. But you have to think for me. What is the code name that you use to know that it's safe to go with him." She told her that it was *April*

Showers bring May flowers. "That's a good one. I love it. All right, Kings is bringing him here. Then we'll head to our house and see what we can do about keeping the two of you safe from now on. I'm under the opinion that we just bury him in the back yard someplace there are red ants, but that's just me."

Skye laughed. It was nervous sounding but not nearly as stressed as before. The police arrived and no one mentioned that he was there for Skye. Amanda Wilson would be safe as well as the owner of the place was going to fire her for leaving in the middle of the shift. Kaida was able to get her out of the place without anyone seeing her.

"I need some juice." There was a juice bar not far from where they were, so she and Skye headed there. "I was told that when I use a lot of magic that I was going to need to have more fruit and juices in me." Kaida babbled on while Skye looked around.

She didn't know if she was worried that someone might recognize her or if she was looking for her son. But when Kings showed up with him in his car, the reunion was tearful. She was glad now that she didn't ignore the need to get out of the house and walk the streets. Kaida was sure that she had saved the woman, for he would have killed her to get to her son.

After heading back to their home, she got herself another glass of juice. She expected Tucker to ask her what she'd been doing, but all he did was ask her if she was all right. She was, she told him, but for being really dry.

He went into the kitchen and brought her back a large pitcher of what looked like orange juice. She nearly drained it in favor of talking. When she was feeling better, she turned and looked at Skye and her son.

"How did you know?" Confused for a second, she asked her what she meant. "About him coming to get me. For all I know, you told him where I was, and when he brought in the—don't answer that. I'm sorry. You wouldn't have risked your life if that had been the issue. But I would like to know how you did that."

"What do you know about the Savage family?" She said that it was reported that they were shifters, dragons of all things. "They're both. Shifters and dragons. I'm mated to Tucker, now married, and with that, I was able to get some of his magic and a bit of my own. When asked by the council, they said that I must have had a dragon sometime in my family, and that's why I can do as many, if not a few, extra things that Tucker can't do. You needing help from me called to me while I was home, and I came to figure it out."

She went on to tell her how she was ready to give up and get some lunch when she bumped into her. Telling her what she got from that small touch. It was Tucker who finished up for her.

"My little dragon called for help, and we came to help her. I've seen Mr. Houston in—" she told them that she'd never been married to Jason, but he'd asked her out, and things went downhill from there. "I'm sorry then. Is Matt his son?"

"No. He's not really mine, either. I was on the run, and so was he. But someone put a flyer out for a million dollars if they were to bring Matt back to them. He said that he didn't know where they were going to get that much money, as they always told him that they were broke."

She looked at the young man, and when he nodded, she continued. "They do have money. A great deal of it. But they only brought Matt around when they had people over for dinner and such. He's very brilliant and can read something once, and he knows it word for word. Other things as well, but he didn't want to be their...he called it a dog and pony show anymore, so he ran away about the same time that I did, and we just clicked."

When dinner was served, the two of them looked as if they were going to sob. Apparently, it was the first hot meal they'd had since getting together and on the run. Even the meal that she got at work, she'd bring it back to the house and share it with him.

After dinner, Tucker made a few calls. They were going to be safe in their home. As soon as she showed them their rooms, she was sure that they could have slept standing up. Since she had no idea how to give magic to someone, Kaida asked Tucker to give them the magic of clothing. Skye said it had been several days since she'd been able to get to the laundromat, and she needed some clean clothing on her back. Everywhere else, she told her too.

She was nearly ready for bed, too, when Matt came to find them. He said that he wanted to talk to them since they'd been so kind as to help him out of the situation that they'd been in.

"My parents are Matthew and Delilah Connor. I'm sure that you've heard of them. They have heard of you." Tucker said that he'd had a few dealings with them, too. "I thought so. They don't have a very high opinion of you and your cousins. You're not old money like they are. I'm not sure where they got that, as I'm sure you're older than this town, but they think that you shouldn't be allowed in respectable places because of how you got your money. How did you get your money?"

"As you guessed, we've been around forever. Made investments in things that were new then but are still around today. Like lumber companies. Computers and phones. You might as well know that we've been the start-up for a lot of things that are going on in his world today. One of them being airplanes." Matt said that he knows about investments as well, and that was what had saved his parents from ruin. "However, I stopped doing that as well when I got smart enough to know that they didn't care if the company was selling shares or not. They were going to invest in it."

"I've heard about that as well. They're being looked at for a couple of murders, too. I wouldn't put it past time to kill, but I don't know them all that well." Matt said that he did and knew that they had done that and more. "I would imagine."

Matt told them of a few other things that he could do as well. "My father figured out that I could see a bit into the future when it came to investments. As far as I know, he never said anything to my mother, but he would beat me regularly when I didn't give him what he wanted. What he never figured out was that not only can I see the futures on a lot of the things they wish to invest in, I can see the ones that fail after a few years, too. Those are the only ones that I would give him. As you can well imagine, they didn't appreciate that too much."

"So this man, Jason, he's been looking for you, and

he just so happened to be looking for Skye as well." Kaida snorted and asked for the real truth as to why she was with him. "I saved her a couple of times. She knows I have some abilities. Whenever Jason gets too close, I can tell her. I messed up this time because I wasn't paying attention to the signs that were given to me. He figured out that she was with me and then that I was the boy who was worth a million dollars. He told me once that he was killing two birds with one pistol. Jason isn't very bright and has a one-track mind. Also, he bets on the ponies, and that is why he's desperate for the money he'll get for turning me in."

Kaida was beginning to see other things, too, that the boy could do. He'd brought a Danish to himself at dinner. Also, his napkin that had fallen in the gravy on his plate was once again clean when he gave it a hard shake. Little things that she had to wonder if the kid even knew he was doing. Looking at him now, she wondered, too, if he realized that he could hide from his family without much in the way of thought.

"I know that." She asked him what he meant. "That I can hide myself away. I could have easily taken all their money, too, but I have to protect Skye. She's the only person that I know who has never expected anything from me other than her friendship. Not to mention, she's been kinder to me than anyone I've ever encountered other than you guys."

"Thank you, young man. You've no idea how much we appreciate that." He nodded and then looked around the room. "What are you looking for. You've been looking around this place since you arrived."

"There are secrets in the walls here that you could

get to. Some of its money and jewels, but there is not just a journal tucked away, but an old bible as well." Tucker asked him if he knew where it was. "I do. It's just above the fireplace and near the pocket doors. I know you have no use for the money that you find, but I have a feeling that the people you brought this house from could use it."

"I'll do that." Matt showed him where each piece of history was hidden. In addition to the things that he'd told them about, there was a bundle of silverware, several more diaries, as well as the first deed to this place that had been built by the family on the original fifty acres. "Are there any pictures of this place?"

"Plenty that have been hidden away as well. There is an old barn out back that you might want to go through as well. You'd be surprised at how much one family can hoard away when they don't want anyone to take it from them. The original name for this place was called Manchester Manor. When you make the improvements on this place, the extra three bedrooms and baths, you'll find a hidden room that is also full of things that were stashed away during the wars."

They'd only just spoken of adding other rooms to the place this morning. It thrilled her that she'd be able to find a bit of history about the place and perhaps put some of the pictures on display around the rooms. She was especially happy to find the old money. She'd frame it up and hang it on the walls as well.

After Matt left them, they headed up to bed as well. Almost too excited to sleep, she curled herself about Tucker's warmth. In the morning, they were going to have to figure out what to do about Matt's parents as well as the man looking for Skye. He needed to be dealt with by one of the dragons, she thought.

Kaida wondered if Skye was mated to any of the cousins. She was disappointed when she realized that they'd all been around her, and no one had said a thing. Maybe they were just supposed to help her. She could do that, too. Help someone who was as down on their luck as she'd been before getting with this family.

Sure, she had a bit of money in the bank, but now she had so much more than currency. She had a love of her life, a home, not a house, as well as magic that she could use to help others. Kaida thought that she could help others all the time if it were as easy as it had been with Skye and Matt. She also knew that this was a rare case and that she wasn't going to have it as easy as she did today. Things just clicked for the two of them.

~*~

"How long will you be gone?" Kings was packing his things as he spoke to them. He told her that he'd be gone for about two weeks, but would have all the investments that they had taken care of. "Taken care of how? And why can't you do that from here?"

"I've been doing it from here. And it's not getting done. I have to go there and have a face-to-face with them so that our money is where it belongs. It's millions of dollars that are tangled up in a weave of lies, and if I don't go now, we may never get it back." She asked him if he needed to go alone. "No. But my cousins are busy. I'd take you with me, but I think that Tucker would have a cow."

He would too. They were having so much fun being a married couple that she couldn't stand for him to be much more than an arm's length away from her before she missed him terribly. Not even explaining to her that they had lifetimes together could she get over the fact that he was going to leave her somewhere. That had come from Kings' parents. His father had said it would only last six months before he'd drop her to the curb. Kaida was very insecure like that.

Taking him to the airport, she felt like she was losing a part of herself. The man was only going to be gone for a couple of weeks, and she was being silly. On the way home, she tried to console herself with thoughts of the party when he returned, but that wasn't working either. She missed him too much. It wasn't as if they didn't have a lot to do while he was gone.

"Matt's parents arrived in town this morning. They're staying at the hotel just outside of town. It's a nice little place, much nicer since it was renovated some years ago." She asked Tucker what the plan was for them. "Nothing yet. It's not like we can keep their son from them. Just keep hiding him away so that they don't do a snatch-and-grab with him. I shudder to think what it is they'd do to him when they find him. They'll more than likely put him under lock and key, and that would be bad for him."

"What about that guy, Jason? What can we do about him?" Tucker told her that he was in jail and would be for a while yet. "I guess opening fire in a restaurant full of people will get your ass in trouble in more ways than one."

"He didn't have any kind of permit to carry either. Not to mention him being a convicted felon who had a gun specification on his record." They stopped just outside of town to pick up some things for dinner. They were having fun feeding Matt. He had the appetite of a full-grown man and the silliness of a child. Plus, he was very intelligent, too.

Thanks to Matt, they knew what his parents looked like. So when they stepped out of the grocery store with a photo in their hand, Tucker stepped back so they'd not have to encounter them. They looked pinched in the face, plus years older than she thought they would be, with a child of Matt's age. She was going to look into that as well.

Keeping an eye on the couple in the parking lot, the two of them picked up the things to make your own Sundays for dessert tonight. They were also having pizzas as it was the cook's night off. She was going to make things for a cookout, but it was Skye who wanted hot pizza right out of the oven, and who could turn that down.

"Excuse me." She turned when someone spoke behind her, and she smiled at the couple. Up close, they looked beaten, like not having their son around was making them lose some grip on their livelihood. Taking the picture when it was shoved at her, she looked at the picture of Matt. It was an old picture taken when he was about seven or so. "Have you seen our grandson?"

She nearly let the cat out of the bag when she nearly asked if he was her son or grandson. Looking at the picture, she could see too that Matt didn't look a bit like his parents, not even an eye color that would maybe make it so that they looked related.

"I don't remember anyone like that. I think that I would too if a child that little was all by himself." She explained that he was ten now and not necessarily hanging out alone. "Oh, so he's with his mother or something? Not that it matters. I've never seen him before."

"Why would you say that?" The woman's voice was sharp and mean. Taking a step back, she told her that she'd not meant anything by it. Only making an observation. "You think that I'm too old to have a son this age? Well, I'm sick of people assuming anything when it comes to him. He's my son, not my grandson, and I don't want to hear another word from you."

They had drawn a crowd now, and she hated that. When Mr. Moore, the store manager, asked her if she was all right, she told him that she was but that the woman seemed out of sorts. As her husband—whoever he was, started pulling her along, Kaida could hear him telling her to hush up before the police were called.

"They've been all over town about three times, whipping out that picture and asking people if they've seen him. I've told her at least a dozen times that I've never seen him. But that doesn't stop her. She's also looking for a woman and a man. I don't know what to think about that, but if you were to ask me, it seems sort of fishy. They're a might too old to be his parents, then all of a sudden today they are his grandparents. What's this world coming to, Mr. Savage?" Mr. Moore shook his head in disgust. Tucker said that he didn't know but would look into it if necessary. "You go on and do that for us. She's being a pain in the ass, pardon my speech, but just look at them every day—I'd probably be doing the same thing if it were my boy. I know that, but why don't they move on? We've done told them that we've never seen him. Now, this man and woman are the ones they're searching for."

"Could it be the same man who shot up Travelers the other day?" It was funny that she was just going to say that when one of the others said it first. "I heard he was looking for a boy, too. You think those people are out to kidnap all our kids? Well, they come around my house, and I'll show them how we greet the door in his town. I'll blow them away."

"Mr. Jacobs, you don't want to be killing anyone. It might be all the stress of losing their son or grandson. I don't know which." No one seemed to have any idea what their names were, either. Kaida thought that odd. To be showing off a picture without any means of contacting them if they were to see the boy. She wanted to race home now and tell Matt what they had discovered, but they needed to be calm about this. Calm and collected until they had more news.

After getting their things bagged up, they headed out the door. Having pizzas tonight seemed slightly spoiled because of the people around town. But she'd bet anything that if Matt were to walk down the main street right now, no one would tell the Connors. She was going to ask him about his grandparents, too.

"I've lived with them all my life, and they told me that I was their son. It never occurred to me that they might be my grandparents until just now." He handed back her phone with a confused look on his face. "How would we find out if they are my parents or not? I mean, not that I ever looked for one, but I never saw a birth certificate when I was living with them."

After getting his birth date and social security number, Brenin started to do a search on him. Coming up with the name of the hospital became something of a trial, as he couldn't remember anyone mentioning that. After about two hours of searching and making pizzas, they had little more information than when they started. Just the name of the hospital that he might have been born in, and a record of his social being used about fifty years before he was born. It was making more questions than answers, she thought.

"I have a plan." Cassian said he wasn't going to tell anyone his plan in the event that it didn't work. She was all right with that, and so was everyone else. About an hour after they'd exhausted every little bit they could find out, one of the members from the local pack came to the house with a bunch of pictures. She worked in the hotel and was a cleaning lady for them.

Getting the information hadn't been all that difficult. All she'd had to have done was go in like she was cleaning, finding the paperwork, and taking pictures. After tidying up the room, she left and finished out her shift. Kaida thought that it was just too easy to get the information from the room and decided that she was going to use the safe in the room when she had something to hide.

"I have DNA, too, that I found in the bathroom. The mister must be a diabetic, and when he pricks his finger, it leaves me enough blood to get some information from that." Kaida shivered, thinking of all the things that were left behind when people stayed at hotels. "I have a friend that I'm sending this off to, and when we get the results back, we'll have a better understanding."

Beth was able to take Matt's DNA, too, and that was sent off as well. Once they got the results back, in a couple of weeks, they were told, then they could work from there. At least they'd know how or even if he was related to the elderly couple at all.

In addition to the things that she located, there were things in the room that had startled her. There were handcuffs as well as chloroform. A body bag, too, that was still in the package. All she could think about now was that she was thrilled that she'd never given them any information when she'd seen them today or the other day. These people weren't right in the head, and she was slightly afraid of what they might do in order to get Matt back to them.

"There is no record of birth filed in the county where he was born. There are no files with the Connors' name on them either. No homes, no driver's license. They have never voted either, as far as I can tell. I can't find a place where they have voted or even registered to vote with their registration on it." She asked what that meant. "They aren't real. At least as far as the county is concerned."

The more they dug, the deeper they were in with questions. If he were their child, there should have been something that would have had his name on it. There wasn't anything. The car that they drove around was a rental, but it wasn't registered to anyone they could find. Just a post office box number that didn't exist either.

Digging into Jason's life. They found more information on him than she could have imagined. He had convictions all up both his arms. Armed Robbery, solicitation, hit and run, as well as kidnapping. That was all there was in the top few of the list, and she sat down at the table.

"How does he keep getting out of jail? It looks to me like he's been let out at least a dozen times after only serving a few weeks. Who is releasing him? And why?" No one had an answer, and she knew that they wouldn't. "It's too bad we don't know anyone with...maybe I can do it."

"Maybe you can do what?" She explained to them how she needed to find Skye and that she'd only had to touch her before she was able to not just figure out who she was, but also that she needed her help. "It's worth a shot. What do you need?"

"I'm not sure. Let me just think about this for a minute." She sat down with all the paperwork that they had on the man and the older couple and started touching things. She could get little bits of information on them but nothing more. When she picked up the DNA package, she felt a swarm of information roll over her until she had to let it go. She looked up at Tucker.

"It's bad, isn't it?" She nodded, and he sat down beside her. "All right. Tell me, and we'll work from there. Or you tell me what I need to do, and I'll do it. I trust you with my life, love, and we can do this together."

Almost as soon as he touched her with his hand, she knew that he was getting all the information that she'd found. Even Matt's real name and that of the people to whom he'd been born.

"They killed them. Like they were nothing, they killed his parents to get to the boy when they found out about how smart he was and what he could do." She nodded and waited for him to continue. "They killed that young couple just because they had a smart son, and they wanted him for his magic."

"Not just that. They wanted his inheritance. However, they were never able to collect on it due to the fact that they'd have to admit who Trevor—his real name, was and how he'd come to be with him. Greed and evilness. If that wasn't enough, they stole all the things that he had at his house and took them with them. Wiping out all evidence of the boy even being there. The couple is buried under their home so that they could keep a good eye on them, never being found."

"Christ." Tucker got up to pace. He was tossing out comments like he was giving this a great deal of thought and tossing them away nearly in the same breath. He was pissed, she could tell that, and worst of all, she didn't know how they could make the Connors pay for what they'd done. "He was only one, so it stands to reason that he'd probably not remember his own parents. Or he does, and that's what is keeping him up at night. I know he has nightmares. I hear him crying out when he goes to sleep."

"We have to do something. I don't know that much about laws to know where to even begin." He said that he might well know someone. "Good. But before we do anything, we're going to have to tell Skye and Trevor what we figured out. And how. It's the least we can do to keep them safe if they know what they're up against."

"I agree." He continued to pace the room, and when he stood in front of her again, she knew that he'd hit on something, but wasn't very happy with it. "If she were a mate to one of my cousins, this would be so much better for her. But they all said that they didn't think she was and—"

"Didn't *think* she was?" He nodded, then smiled. "So there is a chance like you didn't know that she's someone's mate, and they just don't know how to figure it out. Christ, Tucker, if I could find your parents right now, I'd dig them up and kill them again. Who treats their children like they did and think that it's all right?"

"Not just my parents but all of our parents. I think they were sick with money and power, and it went to their head." She agreed with him. "There are a couple of things that I can take care of right now, but in the meantime, you do your thing with whomever you thought could help. Tonight, we'll sit down with Trevor and Skye and tell them what we've figured out. Maybe they'll have some more information once we start telling them what we've figured out."

He kissed her on her mouth and left her there. She wondered if there would ever be a time when she didn't want him to leave her. Things were heating up concerning the young man and his guardian. She only hoped that she could keep them safe until such time that they could figure out if they were mates or not with one of the others.

She liked Skye and hoped that they could be long-lasting friends. If only they could get the things cleared up with the couple and Jason. They were going to have to go and soon. Kaida didn't even care if the lot of them were killed or put into prison, so long as they were out of their lives.

~*~

Skye wasn't sure if what they were telling her was the truth of things, but she also had no reason to not believe them. To think that the boy she'd been taking care of for the last few years wasn't even their son or grandson, and he had magic, too. She wondered for a moment if she had been caring for him or if he was caring for her. It seemed that he was a good deal smarter than she was in all things.

"Are you all right?" She nodded, then shook her head at Matt…Trevor. That was something else she was going to have to get used to. He was Trevor and not Matt, as they'd all thought. "I know just how you feel. It's like my life has been a lie, and I just don't know where to start over or just let things go the way that they are now."

"I'm sorry about your parents, Trevor. They've been so close to you all this time, and you didn't know." He told her that he thought, too, that they'd been watching over him. "I don't doubt that at all. You're a good kid and smart, too. They'd be so proud of you right now."

"You had a lot to do with my upbringing, Skye. I wouldn't have survived those first few years had you not taken me under your wing. You're the best mother figure a kid like me could have." She hugged him. Holding back tears as best she could, she held onto him until he pulled away. It occurred to her that she loved him like he really was her own son and wouldn't have had it any other way. "Don't get all emotional on me. You'll ruin my new shirt."

They both had a lot of new things. Not just clothing, but a room for themselves. Food whenever they wanted it, as well as someone to talk to in the way of the Savage family. All of them had been very good to them, and she couldn't have been happier to have them in their lives.

"Kaida saved my life, and I can't help but feel like I owe her everything. Did you hear that Tucker is looking into some contacts to figure out what to do next? It's not like the Connors are going to be getting out of jail anytime soon. Nor will Jason." They had enough evidence on the Connors to keep them in jail as a flight risk. So far, they had demanded that the police allow them to take their son home and be done with everything. They weren't budging on allowing them to get out anytime soon.

Jason was going back to prison. This time, she hoped for good. The man had murdered more people than she would have imagined. And he'd been hired by the Connors to kill her and take the kid. How they figured out that she was with him, she might never know, but it was scary for her to think what he would have done to her had she not kept on the run from him.

"I think that we're safe for now, don't you?" She said that she'd never felt safer than she was right now. "Good. I was hoping you'd say that. Now, before you get upset with me, I'm going to go and see the Connors. They won't be in the same room as I will be, but far enough away from them that they can't touch me. Tucker said that he thinks I can get a confession from them where no one else will be able to."

"Please don't do this." He said that he needed some closure, too. "I would imagine that you do, but this isn't the way to go. They could hurt you. If not physically, then mentally, for sure."

"I started to tell you that I'd be fine, but I don't know that for sure. I do know that if I don't do this, I'll wonder for the rest of my life as to why and how they did this to them and to me." He hugged her. "You can understand that, can't you? Why I'd need to know what made me so special at such a young age that they thought that they could get away with this. And they might well have if not for you coming along when you did."

They talked about other things in their life rather than the one that was going on now. She understood why he needed this and was happy that he could. However, she didn't have to like it any more than she was going to like confronting Jason someday in court. It was funny—not ha-ha funny, but weird funny—how the two of them had found each other. If they hadn't, she was sure that at some point, she would have been murdered, and Trevor would be right back with the Connors being locked up in his room and only brought out when there was a way to show him off. Her heart hurt for the young boy.

When Tucker left with Trevor a few hours later, she went to the kitchen to find something to munch on until dinner. She didn't know what she was smelling, but she was looking forward to having whatever it was. This house always smelled like home-cooked meals and love. She envied the love that Kaida and Tucker had. It was like they were each in their own little world and only came out when it was impolite not to. She laughed every time she caught them kissing. It would embarrass them so much.

Getting to the police station an hour later, the time being set up by Jason's attorney, she sat outside his cell and watched him fumble around with his clothing. His attorney, someone she'd only just met, told her that she could ask him anything she wanted, but she wasn't to expect it to be used against him. Standing up, she was nearly to the door when she was called back.

"He told me that you'd be stubborn about this. Remember, Ms. Houston, whether he agrees or not with that, everything is being recorded, including the fact that there is a camera in every cell." He winked at her, and she returned to the seat. "Now, she's only here because it was a request of yours to see her, Jason. What is it you wish to talk to her about?"

"Why couldn't you have just died?" Skye was startled by the questions. "It didn't matter what I did about you or to you; you just fucking wouldn't die. Christ, and I really tried, too. Everything that I did, you'd just get up and walk away."

"Maybe you just weren't as good as you thought you were." He said that he'd hired people to kill her, and they couldn't do it either. "I think a better question would be, why did you want me dead? I didn't know you at all. But you kept coming after me like you were stupid or something."

"I am not stupid, you fucking cunt. I've been killing women for decades, and you just wouldn't die." She asked him how many people he had killed. "Not people but lowlifes that owed someone something. I just wanted you dead, then one day, I saw you with that kid. I'd seen his picture someplace and went to the Connors about it. They didn't care what happened to you so long as they could get their boy back. Why did you kidnap their kid?"

"He wasn't their child. They killed his parents to get him." He snorted and told her that was why they were caught. Freelancing with murder is always going to get you caught. "Yet here you sit with bars around you, caught too."

"You can't use this against me. I told you that." She shrugged and told him that she didn't care what he said.

She'd use it if she were asked. "You fucking bitch. I swear to you, I hate people."

"I'm sure that not too many like you either. You're a murderer, a liar, and a thief." She looked at the attorney, and he winked at her. "What did you want to talk to me about? I have a busy schedule and I need to keep on track of it."

"I hired someone to kill you soon. And when they do, I'm going to dance a little dance in happiness. You'll never be able to thrall him as you have me. He's a professional." She told him that he worked for the police. "No, I told you. I hired him right out of the jail cell before he got out."

"Right. He's working now, telling them everything you told them about me. In addition to things that you told him about me, you're also going to be tried for trying to kill off Trevor and the people who hired you to kill him. You tried to get them to pay up, and when they didn't, you—"

"No. He was in the jail cell right there. You don't know what you're talking about." She told him what he looked like. "No, you're wrong. Damn it. I know what I'm talking about." The door opened down the hall, and she glanced in the direction of Brenin. He'd been in the jail cell next to Jason's and had recorded every word of what he wanted done to her. "That's him right there. See? I told... what is he doing here?"

"He's my friend. And when they wanted you to confess to murder for hire, they asked him to come in and pretend to be a gun for hire. Didn't you think it was suspicious that he seemed more up on the laws than you did? Christ, you're an idiot of the first order, aren't you?"

Leaving this time, she let his shouts echo down the hallway where she was headed. Brenin asked her if she was all right, and it was all she could do not to break down and fall on her face. As soon as she was outside, she sat on the steps and put her head between her knees.

"You told me what he said, but I didn't want to believe it. He was going to hire you to kill me." She looked up at him. "I know that you wouldn't have, but just the thought that he thought it was all right to hire someone to come along and kill me simply because he'd been asked to do it. I just don't understand where his mind was."

"He's probably been at killing for a good long time, and since he was never caught, he felt that he was doing something right. At least that's what I'm thinking." She asked him if he'd run into that sort of thing before. "I have. We all have. It's just the way that some people think about themselves. That they're something along the lines of the almighty, and what they say and do is the way things should be done. I'm sorry that he hurt you, honey. Why don't you and I have some dinner and a nice cold beer and enjoy the rest of the day without thinking about Jason?"

She took him up on his offer and wondered if Trevor was doing any better. She hoped so. The young man needed to have a good look on life before he got too much older and was jaded. Like her, he was all alone in the world, and she wanted nothing more than to keep him safe and happy for the rest of their lives.

Chapter 1

Kings, he loved his new nickname, watched after Trevor while they walked around town. The boy meant a great deal to him, and he couldn't believe how much he loved him. He needed to talk with Skye again—he'd been avoiding her—to see if she was his mate or not. It made sense to him that she might be, but he'd been assigned to keep an eye on young Trevor, so he'd not been around her all that much.

He, of all his brothers, didn't mind getting a mate. He didn't care if she was human or not. It had occurred to him that it didn't matter what they were coming into the family; it was when they were a part of it that they really made them shine. And shine they did. He had no doubt that if Skye was his mate, she'd be just as helpful and magical as the other wives of his brothers when they came along.

"What do you suppose possesses a person to open a grocery store?" His first thought was greed, and that's what it had been for people that he'd encountered opening one. Then, when he thought about it, he knew what Trevor wanted as an answer. So he told him. "I don't know. Need? It sort of sounds lame."

"Think about it. The need to have someone put in a grocery store was paramount to the people of the town many years ago. And I'm talking like, well, before you were born. Because it wasn't just a store that sold things like flour and sugar. They also sold stamps, made sure your mail got to you, and when it went out. They were there for news, too. Everyone came into the store and would have a bit of gossip to tell. He'd know it all. So it was a community information center too. Not to mention, he'd know the honest people about as well as the people who gave birth and who died recently. He was a hub of information. A person opening a store had to be handy, organized, as well as someone people could trust."

"I guess I can see that. Not just anyone would be able to juggle all those hats and come out a part of the town. I see that."

They walked around the town looking for nothing at all but seeing things that he'd never noticed before, like the schools. Even though they'd built them when they first got here, they were starting to show wear and tear. He didn't know how long a building was supposed to last, but he'd bet that they should be looking into updating or replacing these again.

There were quite a few buildings that were empty now. Wondering when that had happened, he made a mental note to himself to check on those. Where did the businesses go, and how long had they been gone? More importantly to him was whether someone was keeping track of the buildings that were empty so that someone didn't move into them, taking over the building as their own.

When they were heading back to his home, he told Trevor that the weather was supposed to turn ugly tonight. With rainstorms coming in, there might be some power outages around the town, and that would cause trouble. People would be lighting candles to be able to see, which might cause fires in the homes. They needed to be on the lookout for those.

Once they were home, they had some lunch and made plans for the dinner meal. It was kind of boring living with a kid, he thought all they thought about was food and when the next time they were going to eat. He supposed he might have been the same way, but it had been so long ago now that he could no longer remember. Laughing to himself, he thought about how he could liven things up and decided to go and see what Skye was up to. She was always fun for a nice change of topic.

It took him longer to find her than he thought it should have. She wasn't in the house as he had assumed, nor did she seem to be on the grounds of the property. Reaching out to his cousins, he asked them if they knew where she'd gone and was told that she was having lunch with Kaida. They were going to be working on a project together.

He knew that he couldn't go to the restaurant and cause trouble, so he was stuck at home with Trevor, who was playing on one of the gaming systems that he'd gotten sometime back. Picking up a book, he decided that he could entertain himself by reading a good book. Or a bad one. He didn't care so long as he wasn't bored.

At a bit after four, he heard the front door open and Skye come inside. He also heard Kaida as he was getting out of the chair and went to see what he could get into. His entire body seemed to seize up when he noticed the blood on Skye's face.

"What happened?" Clearing the distance between them, he picked her up in his arms and took her to the couch. "You're covered in blood. Who did this to you? And where do I find them?"

"I did it to myself. Let me go, you moron. I'm fine. It's just a small cut." He examined the cut, then the rest of her face. Finding nothing more than the small cut on her cheek, he demanded again who had hurt her. "I told you. I did it. I was coming around the corner and hit my cheek on the wall. It's no big deal."

The need to have her seen by a professional was making his head spin. Once he figured out that she was going to murder him if he didn't calm the fuck down, he sat back on his knees and came to the conclusion that she was indeed his mate. He told her that.

"Is that a reason for you to become deranged?" He nodded and told her that it was every reason for him to become concerned. "You're not concerned. Concerned is asking me what happened in a calm voice and not picking up like I've broken my ankle. You're deranged. What is up with you?"

"I told you that I belong to you. I'm your mate. Did you notice how I said that? Not that you belonged to me but that I belong to you." She said he was a moron. "Why are you calling me names? I did nothing to you to warrant that."

"Look, can you just back off a second? I need to get my bearings. For days, you ignored me, now you're practically sitting on top of me. Just back off and give me some breathing room." He stood up and backed away to the chair across from the couch he'd put her on. It was too far away from her, so he moved closer until he could touch her. "You're doing it again. Just let me...is this how you're going to be acting all the time?"

"Yes. I want to protect you." She said that the only person she needed protecting from was him. "Now you're just being mean. I'm only within touching distance right now. I'm not all up in your face."

"I give up." She sat up and put her feet on the floor. In order for her to stand, he was going to have to back up again, and he wasn't ready to do that. "So what does this mean? You belong to me? I don't have time for this. I'm trying to keep myself from being killed in the event that might have skipped off in your head."

"He's not going to hurt you again. No one will." She asked what that meant again, and it was Kaida who answered. While she did, he got to observe Skye and look her over. He had forgotten that she was on someone's to-be-killed list, honestly. She'd been hanging out with Kaida and Tucker for so long that it was why it had taken him until today to figure out she was his mate. Or something along those lines. "So you see, you'll be fine so long as you allow me to protect you."

"I've been doing all right by myself, thank you very much." She finally pushed him away with her feet on the chair. "You're too close. Can't you go back to whatever you were doing before you realized this thing about us being mates? I think I liked you better then."

"I was reading a book. It wasn't all that good, but I was caught up in the plot. It's a good murder who done it." She asked him who had written it, and he said he didn't know, he'd forgotten to look. At least when she was talking about the book, she wasn't calling him names. Kings didn't know why, but it hurt his heart a little when she did that. Like he had done something terribly wrong and she was scolding him about it. "What can I do for you to make you like me better?"

"Back off. Something that I've been saying to you since I came in here. Where's Trevor? Aren't you supposed to be watching him? He's a bigger target than I am." He told her that nothing would harm him either. They were both under his protection. "We'll see about that."

"I'm glad you're his mate. Now you can be a part of my family. I don't have any women friends." Kaida hugged Skye and then sat down on the couch. "You should ask her what we got done today. We had a very productive day in getting things organized for the upcoming street fair that is going on in August."

The two of them talked about the street fair and how it was going to benefit so many things this coming fall. Usually, he and his cousins donate money to the school to get backpacks for the kids who couldn't afford them. But this year, they were also going to load them up with things that they could use. It sounded like they had lists for each grade and were going to purchase the things and load up the backpacks for the grades. They were only going to do about ten per room, and that would leave the rest for the parents to do. He didn't know how that was going to work out; people could be jealous of things like that happening, and they weren't a part of it. He told them that.

"What would you do then? I mean, there are a lot of families that can't afford the supplies that are needed to get through the class year." He said that he'd need more time and information about it before he could make a decision. "Backpacks are nice and all, but they don't do them any good if they can't get the supplies to fill them."

"Your way is going to have parents that might well have afforded it, not buy them because they know that someone down the street is getting one for free. That's all I'm saying. It has to be fair or people are going to get upset." She asked why they didn't do this before. "For that very reason. While we can afford it, it's still draining on us to have to go out and get the supplies for each classroom, and they're all different, so that the few that can't afford it can have supplies while the others can. Understand?"

"I guess I do. It would be like having your wallet out for every little project and plan they have going on. And then they'll be wanting bigger projects to be paid for by us. It'll get expensive, and no one will have anything special done for them because they've all gotten something for nothing." Skye nodded and continued. "Yes, I understand that. I never thought beyond making things better for those who don't have the funds. I should have realized what other people would feel about that."

"We've been around for a long time, and we've experienced it all, I think. We've tried to be helpful in other towns that we've lived in, and the result was the same. We've learned a great deal in coming here and just bargaining with the people who live here, like for the computers to be used in the library. We matched them dollar for dollar on getting four of them. They ended up with eight nice computers and printers for the library. As I said, we've been around for a very long time and have learned a great deal over the years. What we've done in the past is buy a bunch of backpacks and let the kids pick out the ones that they want. Anything left over is held until the next year, and that's worked out great for us. That way we've helped out and it helps all the stores around too because we buy them at retail price from the local stores and they make out as well."

"I guess that'll work out because it does every year." Both women seemed to be upset with his plan, but he knew that it was the one that worked out best for everyone. "What do you do for the teachers? I'm sure they could use some help, too."

"Three times a year, we hold a contest about who has the best grades going forward. It's not just the kids, but the teachers are graded as well. The principal will notice things that are going on in the classrooms or on the playground that he wants to nominate a teacher for, and their names are put into a bucket and pulled out. The more you do for your class, the more times you get your name in the bucket. The teachers can win five thousand dollars if they win each time. There are second and third-place winners as well. It's been going over very well, and there are a lot of teachers who stay because of the money they can win. And they don't have to use it for the classroom, either. It's their winnings."

"We should have spoken to you before we had lunch. I feel like it was a total waste of time." He asked if they'd had fun too. "Well, yes, whenever you get a group of women together, there is always fun to be had. It's why we do it."

"Then it was a well-spent afternoon. You did learn

something, too, so that's not all bad." Skye eyed him sharply. "Now what did I do wrong?"

"You made it sound like we learned a lesson that made us sound like failures." He told her that she was just looking for things to be mad at him about. "No, I'm not. Because we didn't ask the mighty dragons, we had to learn a lesson that you know better."

"Even I think you're reaching there, Skye. He didn't mean that at all." Kaida stood up and announced that she was leaving. "You, too, will have to work this out, and when you do, let me know. I love a good fight, but this is just being picky. Goodbye, all."

When she left, Kings looked at Skye. She looked upset, but rather than ask her what was going on in her head at that moment, he kept his mouth shut and stood himself. He didn't have anything going on that needed his attention right now, but he also didn't want to get into a fight either. He'd just found his mate, and he didn't want to spend the rest of his day bickering with her over nothing.

Finding Trevor in the kitchen, the two of them decided to have Chinese for dinner. They'd order from the local place and go pick it up, or they'd just go there. It was left up to Skye to decide what she wanted to do. Trevor said that he'd do the asking as he'd heard a little bit of the argument that the two of them had been having.

~*~

Skye enjoyed her dinner and was happy for the company, too. The two of them were going out of their way to make her happy, and while she appreciated it, she hated that she'd been snipping at Kings so much. There was no reason for her to take her worry out on him.

He did seem to be in a good mood, which helped her mood. She didn't know what was wrong with her about him, but he was just too much. Christ, he looked as if he lifted trees out of the ground to curl them, and he, while mannered, ate like he was eating for the entire family instead of one big man. There she was again, picking at him.

"What else did you learn at your luncheon?" She asked him what he meant and then apologized to him. She told him she didn't know what was wrong with her. "You do seem to be out of sorts. I only meant, did you learn anything about the school that we're helping? Kaida seems to know a great deal about a lot of things, and I wondered what she told you. I was noticing the school seemed to be getting worn down."

"We did talk about the school." She told him how they had discussed that the teachers were all new this year; thankfully, that was so, as they had been several teachers short at the end of the last year. Also, while they did talk about the school, they'd gotten a grant this year for new updates to the computers that are used in the classes. "They can all use a smart board now, and the teachers seem to really like it. It's big enough for all the kids to see around the room, I was told."

The three of them talked about Trevor going to school so long as the Connors weren't around anymore, nor Jason Waggoner either. The Connors had killed Trevor's parents when he'd been about one year old to steal the kid. He could do things like predict the outcome of investments, and they wanted to show him off to their friends when they came around. Otherwise, he was locked in his room without any way to talk to anyone but them. He thought they were his parents and didn't remember his own mom and dad.

Jason had wanted Skye to be his wife and was chasing her all over Ohio to catch her. When he'd seen the boy, he realized that he could get two for one—the Connors were putting out a huge reward to get Trevor back. When he'd come into the restaurant that she'd been working in, waving a gun around and firing it into the ceiling, he was arrested for that. He had then confessed to killing lots of people, and the police were awaiting trial for him so that he could be sent away to prison. Just where the Connors were headed for murder and kidnapping.

"I was in fifth grade, but I was bored. I would like to take some classes online so that I can get a jump on my college education." Skye said that they could look into that. "Good. Also, I know that I can be tested to be out of some of the grades that I can go to, but I don't want to do that. I'd like to remain in the grades that I'm supposed to be in for my age. I don't think I'd do well in a class setting with kids that are a lot older than I am."

"We can look into that, too. The local pack has a good school that teaches based on the level of your intelligence rather than your age." Trevor said he'd like to give that a shot. "Good. I'll talk to them in the morning to see what needs to be done. You'd be safer there, too, with the pack around you all the time."

"I'm excited about this." Kings said he could tell and was glad that he'd been able to help. The best part was that Skye didn't get upset with him this time. Maybe she was just out of sorts earlier. "Do they take humans?"

"You're far from human, Trevor." He agreed with Skye. "You've more magic than I think some of the pack will have. Just be careful there. And watch yourself. You don't want to be caught up in the same situation that you were with the Connors."

"No. You're right. I don't want that again." Trevor looked at him. "You've given some magic to Skye, haven't you? I can almost taste it on her."

Before she could get upset, and she looked like she was going to go that far, Kings put up his hand. Telling them that he'd not given her anything of the sort, but then he explained how she'd gotten some.

"Just by being my mate, you got some magic. Also, when you hugged Kaida today, I'm sure she gave you some of hers without knowing. Being around Tucker and the rest of the cousins means you'll get even more because you'll be related to them by being my mate. I didn't give you anything physically. It just came to you to keep you safe." She asked what kind she might have, already less upset about it now that he had explained. "I would imagine that you can change your clothing at will. Also, Kaida has some powers that Tucker didn't have before she met him. He has them now, but on a larger scale. She's pretty powerful, and so is Tucker, so there is no telling what the two of you will get from them."

"I'll get power too?" He said that he already considered him his son, so he didn't see why not. "Thank you for that. You've been a better dad to me than the Connors were. And Skye has been the best mom. Even though I have some power of my own, she's been protecting me since we got together all those years ago.

The three of them spent the rest of the evening talking about magic. Skye could change her clothing at will, and so could Trevor. It was the most basic skill he told them, and said how it came in handy at times, too. Skye could touch something and feel a connection to it. She could tell where it had come from and who had owned it. That wasn't a great skill, but she was thrilled with it and, by extension, so was he.

Later that night, when they were headed to bed, he asked Skye what room she wanted in the house. Since she'd never been here other than to meet up with Trevor, she had no idea. He told her to take the master as he'd never slept in there either. She seemed hesitant at first, but after telling her that he wanted her to have it, he made his way down to the bedroom that he'd been sleeping in since buying the house.

It was a grand room. Almost as big as the master, it also had a window that showed off the back yard nicely. Not only was there a view of the back yard, but there was a smallish deck that was out from the window that afforded him great views of the pool and pool house. He loved the room and hoped someday that he could convince Skye that it made a better master suite than the one she was sleeping in.

Getting ready for bed, he brushed his teeth again and set up his clothing for the morning. Yes, he could change his clothing as well, but he liked knowing when he went to bed what he was going to be wearing the next day. It was something that he did all his life, and he didn't see any reason to stop doing it now that he had the magic.

Tomorrow he had a meeting with Cassian, and he was looking forward to it. They'd been meeting together once a week for years now, and again, he saw no reason to forfeit his time with him because he had a mate. She'd no doubt be going out with Kaida and the other women when they came around, so he thought it would be good for him to meet with his cousin.

He and the others met once a month. All four of them getting together to catch up. They might well see each other a few times during the day, but it was nice to actually have a seat with them and catch up on things that didn't seem all that important until you shared them with the others. It was his favorite time of the month to have his cousins all with him when they got together.

Getting into bed, he was surprised at how tired he was. He'd been doing a lot of walking with Trevor lately, and that could have been it. Also, he'd been using the gym equipment he'd gotten when he moved into his new home, and that was making both him and his dragon feel better. He thought that he was even sleeping better than he had before.

Rolling to his side, he thought of Skye being his mate and wondered what that would bring into his life. He knew that it was going to be a big change for her and was looking forward to the changes for them both. He still had some work that he was doing. Not daily, but enough that he wasn't home all the time. He'd noticed that that sort of arrangement was the kind that Tucker and Kaida had. Where they went their separate ways daily, only to meet up later for whatever they would do. He was sure it was plenty of sex, but he'd never ask, not that he thought anyone would tell him. And he was glad for that, too. Sometimes, information could be too much.

Waking in the middle of the night, he wasn't sure what woke him. It wasn't until he heard a scream that he thought that it was ongoing. Getting up and running to the master suite, he was terrified to find Skye missing. It wasn't until Trevor turned on the light that he found her curled up in a tight ball in the corner of the room. Her crying was tearing at his heart something terrible.

"I have you, Skye." She fought him until he could get her to understand that she was safe and that he had her. Picking her up from the floor, he took her back to the bed and laid her gently on it. "There's nothing here. I have you. Come on now. I have you. Tell me what scared you."

"Jason was getting me." He told her that he was in jail and not getting out anytime soon, so she was safe. "I think it was the new room and all. I thought about how safe I was feeling when I turned off the light, and that must have triggered a memory of him finally catching up with me. He was going to kill me."

"He won't now. I have you." He told her, too, about being immortal, and that seemed to have had a positive effect on her bad dreams. "You can't be killed, either of you, unless they remove your head. And I doubt very much he'd do that."

"Knowing him, he'd do it just to prove that he's killed me." Trevor said he was headed back to bed. "Good. I'm sorry that I woke you. I've not had a nightmare like this for some time now. Like I said, I think it was the new room and my thoughts before going to sleep."

Kings held her until she fell asleep again. Putting

her back under the covers gave him a little fear when he thought that he saw a shadow of blood on her leg. It turned out that she was wearing blood red socks on her feet, and he had to laugh about that. She must have cold feet like he did sometimes.

Going back to his room after getting the lights off again, he didn't know if he'd be able to sleep now. Instead of getting into bed right away, he opened up his computer and looked at information on school buildings and how long they lasted. When he'd bored himself enough, he climbed into bed and got comfy again. It was going to be a long day tomorrow if he didn't get some sleep. Happy that Skye felt safe enough to fall asleep in his arms, he closed his eyes and fell back to sleep.

Waking again just as the sun was coming up, he got up and took a long, hot shower. His feet were giving him fits because they were cold, so he put on some wool socks to go out into the day. After leaving a note in the kitchen about the interviews that were going on today, he told Skye and Trevor that he'd be back before noon, then he was having dinner with his cousin at six.

The house wasn't as large as the last one he'd had, but they would need staff. With the two of them working, even if it was only part-time, the house would suffer. Plus, he didn't want to have to cook all the time, and he was sure that Skye had better things to do than cook, so they'd need someone to come in and do that for them. He thought staff enough to come in and make the beds would be nice too. He didn't enjoy that task as much as some people did and would love the help to get it done.

As he started out his day, he found himself

whistling. It was an odd tune that he'd heard long ago, but he was feeling pretty good and didn't mind having a tune in his head. Smiling at the first person he met today, Kings thought he could get used to having a mate. It was life-changing.

Chapter 2

Trevor walked around the classroom and enjoyed what was going on. There were classes that he could take and enjoy, so he was hoping that he would be able to go here with the permission of the pack master, Jamison 'J.J.' Jenkins. When asked if he wanted to sit in on a couple of classes, Kings said it would be fine with him; he'd be outside. After that, he sat in on two classes on how to survive in the outdoors. He enjoyed them a great deal and learned a lot.

"You ready to go here?" Trevor could barely contain his excitement and nodded rather than make a fool of himself laughing. "Good. It's all set up for you. You can start in the incoming year. They run classes year-round, so you can even take a couple in the summer months should you want to. And they'll work with you on the classes that you want to take online."

"Great." On the way home, all he could talk about was what he learned today. It wasn't just survival that he learned, but he'd also made a couple of friends who were his age. Most of the time, kids his age didn't want to hang out with a nerdy guy like him, but they seemed to be just as nerdy as he was. "What kind of relationship do you have with the pack master? I mean, he's not going to charge you too much for allowing me to go there, will he?"

"No. We discussed the price, and it seems too cheap

to me, but then I've never put a kid in school before. He gave me a rundown of things that you're going to need, such as a compass and a survival knife. I didn't know what that was, but he explained it well enough that I think I can find it. There isn't a uniform, but he said that you can wear jeans and a shirt. One that you, for the most part, don't care about, as it will more than likely get dirty while training in the woods." He said one of the other boys said that they camp out overnight. "Yes, you'll not need a tent, but you will need a sleeping bag for the first few overnight trips. Then you'll have to survive on your own after that."

They talked about everything that Kings had been told and what he'd learned at the packhouse. They also talked about how he'd get there and come home. Kings didn't want him traveling alone until they were sure what was going to be happening with Jason and the Connors.

"They might be in jail, but there might be a time when they're released. We might not hear about it until it's too late to make sure that you're all right." He took the fact that they might be released very seriously. He never wanted to be around them if he could help it. And he said as much to Kings. "I don't either. Maybe when you have a few of the classes under your belt, you can hide out from them better, but until then, we'll keep you safe as we can."

It was nearly noon when they returned to the house. He was starving, and Kings made him a healthy snack to hold him over until lunch was finished. He called it healthy, but it wasn't. He'd been given a plate of cookies with the knowledge that he wasn't to tell Skye unless under threat of death. He enjoyed the cookies a great deal more because it was such a fun way to have them.

Skye joined them for lunch, and they told her everything that they learned about the school. Trevor remembered things better this time in the telling because he'd had time to think about it. The following school term started in two weeks, and it was going to be up to him to figure out if he wanted to go then or wait three months for the following classes. Of course, he decided to go to the one in two weeks. Which didn't give them a lot of time to get the things that he was going to need.

Bringing his own laptop was going to be all right with the teacher. Though if he had any games on it, he wasn't supposed to play with them during class. Trevor didn't have any games on his computer, but he also knew that since education was so important to him, he'd not play on them if he did. He loved learning and was looking forward to getting his education started again after being on the run for so long.

Skye had done a good job of keeping his head in the game of learning when they were on the run. She'd check out books for him to read, then she'd quiz him on them. He'd also learned a lot about the human race while running, and not all of it was good. Trevor thought that if they had been running for much longer, he might well have hated people as much as he loved Skye. And he loved her a great deal.

Heading to Columbus in the morning, he had a list that he'd gotten from one of the boys in his classroom. He would need a backpack that was made of something heavier than the ones he'd taken to classes when he'd been allowed to go while living in the Connors' home. He was excited to learn how to pack his gear up and go at a moment's notice.

Boots were something else that he was going to need. They needed to be waterproof and sturdy. He didn't know what that might mean to him, but Kings seemed to understand the mission and was right on board with him getting the best pair that they could find. Something that Kings had told him was that shoes were going to be his best friend when walking a great deal, and he needed to spend money on them to keep his feet dry, warm, and without blisters. Trevor liked that idea too.

As soon as he purchased his boots, he put them on to wear them in. They needed to be good to his feet, and in order to do that, they needed to be broken in. And at first it was kind of exciting, but after a while his feet began to ache because they were so heavy and stiff. But he told himself that he needed to get used to them.

They had dinner in Columbus when they were finished shopping. He was never so happy to get off his feet as he was that night. As soon as he sat down, he knew that he was going to have to check out his feet because they hurt so bad. Going to the bathroom, he was thrilled that he only had a sore spot on his toe and nothing more. He didn't want to put them back on yet, and Kings agreed with him. He felt like he was walking on clouds when he put his tennis shoes back on; they were so much lighter.

Trevor was ready to sleep standing up before they left the restaurant. He knew it was because he'd been so excited, and he wasn't used to walking around so much. It felt like they'd been to fifty stores looking for things, and he was tuckered out. Trying to stay awake on the drive home, all he did was make himself dizzy. So he finally let himself fall asleep before they left the big city and were headed home.

After getting a shower the next morning, his feet were a little sore, as were his legs, but he wore the boots in favor of getting them broken in. They didn't feel as tight today, which was a good thing, but he still had a lot of things that he needed to get. The knife had been his first purchase, and he was learning how to open it with someone around him so if he did cut himself, someone would be there to help him out. So far, so good, he told himself that he'd only nicked himself a little when he was trying to close it back up.

"I got a call from JJ this morning. He said to remind you that you'll need to get yourself some matches or a lighter that you know how to use." He said he'd forgotten about that. "No big deal. He said your first lesson would be learning how to start a smokeless fire and how to keep it going."

Along with his knife, he'd been told that he'd need a small hatchet and some rope. Since they didn't know what kind of rope he'd need, they put that off in favor of him getting to see what the others were using. Also, he was going to need some rain gear. Something that they couldn't find in all the stores that they'd gone to.

He was glad that he'd spoken to one of the boys in his class, or he would have gotten the wrong sleeping bag. He was supposed to get one that was rated for cold weather and small. A tight bag so he wouldn't overload his pack. Skye had wanted him to get the biggest one they had so that he'd be warm. She was looking for him to be comfortable, and he wanted what the others had. It had been a toss-up in who was going to win that argument until Kings stepped in and said it was better for him to have what the others had so that he'd fit in. Skye didn't like it, but she agreed with him. He just hoped that he wouldn't freeze to death while out in the winter months.

Regular school supplies were also something that he was going to need. Pens and paper, of course, and he'd need colored pencils as well as some mathematical things that he could use for his advanced classes that he was going to be able to take. His excitement was hard to contain, but he managed to make sure that he didn't get too excited and have people make fun of him. He thought that the family wouldn't do that, but he was used to others who didn't know him all that well making fun of him about everything.

The morning of school starting was fast approaching. It had him counting down the hours before he was to go. The arrangements had been made for Kings to take him and for one of his brothers to pick him up on the way home. Skye had a bodyguard as well. It was all because they didn't know from day to day what was going to happen with the three people who had chased them forever, with one of them wanting them both dead.

Since the morning of his first class dawned with rain in the forecast, he knew they were going to cancel classes for the day. But as soon as he arrived, they told him that since you could never predict when you were going to have to have something to do with the outdoors, then you would learn more on the rainy days that came to them. Setting out for the first experience of the day, Trevor had to keep telling himself to calm down and to watch what he was doing. He just knew that he was either going to set fire to his sleeping bag or cut his fingers off when trying to open his knife.

He did learn a great deal on the first day. He learned that he was a good deal smarter than he thought he was, and he was a good deal dumber than he thought, too. Learning was fun for him, but he did have to curb his enthusiasm a great deal and not get anyone hurt who was learning, too. He couldn't do it all, though there were things that came to him like second nature. He just needed to sort the differences and make himself a better survivalist.

On his way home with Brenin, they talked about his day. If he were honest with the older dragon, he would have told him all he wanted to do was go home, take a shower, and go to bed. He was that worn out. As soon as he was back at the house, he did take a hot shower but waited up for Kings and Skye to make it home. He was beginning to see the need for him to get into better shape, as he'd not been like he'd thought he was.

By the time dinner was over, he was ready for bed. There was no way that he was going to make it for the rest of the week if he didn't get to bed and soon. Dragging his butt up to bed, all he could think about was how he'd thought he was going to come right home and have some fun telling Skye and Kings what he'd done that day. As it was, all he could do was grunt and groan about his day. Kings was the one who had made sure he got to bed after brushing his teeth.

Not only did he have a hard time getting up the next morning, but he seriously considered skipping school to spend the day in the hot tub that had been delivered. But he knew that he had to be serious about this, or he might as well need to know how to survive and not be able to do it. Starting the weekend, he was going to make himself get on the treadmill and walk at least a mile a day until he could get his energy up and be able to go five like he did the first day he'd been in school. He didn't whine that first day, but boy oh boy did he want to.

Today was just classroom stuff, and he was glad that he hadn't skipped out on learning. He was sore, and it made him feel good, too, that the other two guys in his nerdy class weren't in any better shape than he was. Getting himself in shape might take him a while, but luckily for him, Kings had a gym in the house that he was free to use. Otherwise, he'd have to run in the open like Travis and Burt did when they wanted to work out. He didn't want people to see him when he was starting out working out because they'd make fun of him. He was sure about that.

~*~

"I thought for sure he was going to quit that first day. He's come a long way in getting himself in shape for these trips. I was going to cut them some slack to make sure that they weren't too sore, but Haley, my wife, said that they have to learn, and cutting them some slack would only make it take longer for them to get into better shape." Kings was so happy to hear that he wasn't getting special treatment while in the pack school. He was proud of Trevor for his working it out, but he was more so when he heard that he was encouraging the other two to get into shape, too. "If he were to get himself in a situation where he needed to depend on his wits, I think that he'd come out all right. He might slip up a little, but he'd get there in the end. And his skill at finding food when they need it was better than anyone I've ever seen. He's a good boy and working out much better than I thought he would after that first day."

"He gives us more than grunts when we ask him something now. Just the other morning, he spoke to us like he used to. I've been so impressed with his workout program that I've started using it myself. He's been doing a good job with that, too." JJ said he should be proud of the young man. "Oh, I am. More than I think you could guess. He's come a long way, like you said, but it's been hard on him. But he's never given up. Which goes to show you what sort of man he'll be, I think."

They talked about his grades and how well he was doing in his math and other subjects. He'd been excelling in his English class and had begun helping the others in the class who were struggling. That made him proud, too. In the short four months that he'd been going to the pack school room for classes, he'd come a long way.

"What do you know about the others who were wanting to get at him? The Connors were set to go on trial soon, weren't they?" He told him that they were going to the pre-trial in the morning, as a matter of fact. "I'm hoping that you get some closure on this stuff. I mean, they've admitted to murdering his parents. What more do you think they're going to need to get them out of jail and into prison where they belong?"

"I couldn't tell you. I was an attorney at one time, but it's been too long for me to have to depend on my memory on how that would work for them. I do know that Waggoner is having fits about being in jail while Skye isn't. He seems to think that he can make up a big story about her kidnapping Trevor from the Conners and that will somehow lessen his time in jail." Kings laughed. "So far, all he's done is piss off every officer in the jailhouse with his bad mouthing about Skye. It helps that she goes by there once a day to bring them muffins for having to put up with Waggoner. She doesn't ask about the trial or anything, just wishes them a better day because they have to watch over the idiot. That's what she calls him, too. The idiot. Good name for him, too, if you ask me."

They talked about the upcoming school year for the human children and how it was going so far. He told JJ about the backpacks that were there for them and who would be getting them before he was called away. Kings made his way back home, whistling to himself and being proud of Trevor for what he was accomplishing in the classes he was taking. He couldn't wait to tell Skye.

He'd been thinking a great deal about Skye and her living in the house with him and Trevor. She wasn't just sleeping there but had been observed at running the vacuum too. Yesterday, he'd made dinner for them as it was the cook's night off, and she insisted that she and Trevor clean up. It was a good way for the two of them to talk, too, her and Trevor.

They were getting along well. He didn't talk to her about going to the next level in their relationship, nor did she. He wanted to in the worst sort of way; every time he saw her dressed in her working clothes of a skirt and blouse, he wanted to see how far he could get with her before she told him no. And while he was sure she'd tell him that, every part of his body and mind wanted her to jump his bones and make love for three straight nights or until one of them died. He was more than willing to die for the cause; he just needed her to be a willing partner in it.

Tonight they were going to grill out, and he was looking forward to that more than he had anything they'd been having the last few nights. Steak and baked potatoes with a side of mushrooms and onions. His favorite meal.

It took him most of the morning after taking Trevor to school to get the paperwork gone over for the new buildings they were having put in. They were also going to go over the school with someone to tell them if it would be cheaper to bring it up to code again or just build new. He was all for building new because there wasn't as much back and forth to get it done. Just demo the old building and put in the new one. Done and done, he thought.

It was about noon when Cassian showed up with the blueprints for the new administrative building that was going in for the schools. They'd been working from an old gas station for years, and they were sorely outgrowing it. He looked them over and approved them, but since his brother didn't leave right away, he figured that he had something to say about them. Waiting on Cassian wasn't quick work. He had to have everything perfect in his head before he'd utter a single word about what was bothering him.

"I don't want to do this anymore." Kings leaned back in his chair and waited for him to continue. "I'm sick of doing things for the town, and they never even say thanks anymore. They used to. When we started out helping them with projects, they were always thanking us. But now it's like they've decided that they don't need to tell us anymore. And I, for one, would like to hear it once in a while." Kings asked him who hadn't said it to him today. "The mayor. She's doing a good job but when I went by there with the specs on the new admin building, at first she acted like she had better things to do than to speak to me then she rushed me through a meeting, one that I had set up to talk to her about and then shoved me out the door and onto the sidewalk like I was a pest or something."

"Do you know what today is?" He said it was Wednesday. "Other than that, what started up today? Something to do with kids. And I think if I remember correctly, her firstborn has started today."

"You mean the start of school. I didn't know she had kids." Kings told him that she had four, but only the oldest was starting school today. "So I should have known that and cut her some slack about my meeting."

"I'd say she's pretty distracted, being a single mom and her oldest is starting school today, so she more than likely had to miss a meeting with you. Or someone else who had an early appointment with her today." He said his meeting was at nine-thirty. "About the time the bus would have picked up her son. It couldn't have been easy for her to leave him with the neighbors while she had to run to work."

"How the hell did you know so much about the mayor and her offspring?" He told him. "Oh. I didn't know that she had called you instead of me when she was wanting to apologize to me about this morning. She could have explained about her son, and I would have changed my time."

"She is a professional and didn't want to seem less so to us about her crying about how she'd treated you this morning." Cassian asked if he should call her back. "I wouldn't have cared if she had just explained to me what was going on. Hell, I'm hoping that someday I have that exact same problem. You did it, too, didn't you? Had to take Trevor to school."

"I did, and since he's older, if I had broken down like I almost did, I don't think that he would have ever forgiven me. On the way home, I was a blithering idiot. I'm just happy that I didn't have a meeting with anyone, or I might not have been as nice as she seemed to be when I had a kid to go to school. It's hard. Harder than anything that I've done with him so far, and he's a kid, not a little boy."

"I'm going to call her and explain about how she should have told me. I really would have been all right with her changing the appointment time, no problem." While his brother made his call, Kings got the blueprint approved and signed off on, and sent it to the architect to start on it as soon as possible. Now, if everything else were so easy to get taken care of. Cassian came back to his office with a watery smile on his face. "I shouldn't have been upset. I'm going to make sure from now on that I have it on my calendar when school starts so that I can avoid such calls in the future. That was difficult to talk to her without joining her in her tears. I'm a sap."

"Nah, you're just a man with a big heart." They talked a bit more about the major projects coming up and decided they were going to do some groundwork before going ahead with the inspection of the schools. They, at this point, had no idea what sort of things needed to be updated or upgraded, and didn't want to confuse the terms. "Upgraded would be all the computer systems and the things that the teachers use for teaching. Updating would mean that the entire school, including the grounds and the things that keep the building from falling down on their heads. We need to figure out what needs to be done and what can be put off for a few more years."

"I'm all for that." They did talk about the new influx of teachers who were coming in to teach this year. At the end of the last year, they had three teachers retire, and two of them went off for an extended maternity leave. Since the school system was so up-to-date and well-maintained, it wasn't difficult to get teachers to come here for the kids. "Also, we need to make sure that they'll have background checks made on all of them. We don't want what happened at the other school district to happen here. We need those checks."

The football coach had a felony against him and was to be prevented from teaching at any school. Also, one of the teachers in another district had trouble with the law about their babysitter. The woman had been dating the underage young man since he started working for her. It was a huge scandal that cost the district a huge fine for not doing proper checks on the people who worked for them.

As dinner time rolled around, he was happy to notice that they got a lot more done than he thought they would have. Some of the things that he'd earmarked for tomorrow to get a jump on were finished up, and his entire morning was cleared thanks to his brother's help today. After Cassian left for lunch and returned, he brought Tucker back with him, and they were able to get everything on their calendar finished off, and some of the things for the next day. It meant that he'd be able to sleep past six in the morning tomorrow, and he was thrilled about that. He never got to sleep in.

"Why don't we all have dinner tonight. Kaida and I would love it if you guys were to come over for some steaks on the grill so that we can celebrate the day. It's not all the time that we can get so much work done in one afternoon that we don't have to start early in the morning." They all laughed because it was true, and that it was because having Tucker there had made things go faster, as they didn't have to run him down for answers when they needed him. "Bring Skye and Trevor too. We'll make a family night of it."

"I'll have to ask her. I know she had plans for the day, but I'm not sure how much she might well have been able to get done by herself." Tucker said that she'd been with Kaida all day, so maybe they had just as much luck. "I'll ask her now. For all we know, we might have both had a good day."

It turned out that the woman had gotten a lot done. They'd done several background checks today that came back positive, and one that didn't. It hadn't mattered a great deal on the one that didn't come back with a good record, as she was only going to be a secondary teacher for the third-grade class, and she wasn't needed. But they'd keep her name on file just in case it ever came up again about her working with the school district.

He'd forgotten that Trevor couldn't come over, as he'd had a night experience with the pack. He'd been looking forward to it for weeks now, and they didn't want to disappoint him about the dinner. They'd have plenty more dinners together, but his first camping trip was going to be epic for the young man. Kings wished he could have joined them; that's how excited Trevor had made it sound when he talked about it.

Dinner was as it always was. Loud, fun, and loud. They were a very loud group when together, but they had fun too. As soon as they all sat down to dinner, they talked about their day and not what they'd done today. It was a good time for all of them, and he wouldn't trade his family for anyone in the world.

Chapter 3

Tank looked over the family tree again and couldn't believe what he was seeing. Their last name was Savage, but he never in a million years thought that they'd be related to the Savages that had been around for thousands of years. He asked his brother Ace to look at it so that he could see the same thing that his brother was seeing.

"What am I looking at?" He explained to him about the DNA tests they'd done in order to be qualified for their Private Investigators Licenses. He didn't think that every city or state wanted the tests to be done. It was just his town that decided that they wanted DNA tests done on everyone who applied for city funding or city help with their job—such as police, detectives, and fire departments—to be done. "So you matched up our names with the dragon Savages and came up with a hit. How close are we to being related to them? I don't understand what this means."

"We're cousins." He'd never thought that they'd be related simply because they weren't dragons. They'd been born from an egg, but since their mother was human and their father only half dragon, they were just, as Ace called them, souped-up people with a shit ton of magic. And they did seem to have a great deal of it when it came to needing to use it. "We're related to them by our father being their cousin. Not close cousins, but it doesn't matter;

we're related to them. Isn't that cool?"

"Not to be a bastard about this, but what does that have to do with anything? It's doubtful that they'd care if we were related to them or not." Tank asked his brother why he thought that. "Because dear brother, they've been around for thousands of years, and we've been around for about fifty. Not even that, if you don't count the time since we were hatchlings. Is that what we're called, even though we weren't born dragons?"

"I have no idea. But we did hatch, so I'm thinking that calling us hatchlings is the way to go." Tank looked over the family tree again and smiled. "I wonder what they'd say if we were to go up to them and tell them who we are. I've heard that some of the family members are real bastards and bitches. They'd probably want us to go away, never to return."

"All good reasons not to find them and tell them." Tank looked at Ace, and he shook his head. "No. Please tell me that you didn't contact them already without talking it over with me first. Please tell me that you didn't just open up a can of worms that we have no way to put back."

"You're funny when you're upset. But no, I didn't contact them. The DNA group does that for you. When someone is related to you they let them know that they can contact them for any reason they want. So no, I didn't do that, but it was done. Or is going to be done, I'm not sure how that works actually." Ace asked what they were supposed to do if they contacted them. "I don't know what we're supposed to do other than to be polite and answer them back. For all we know, the rumors about them aren't true, and they're the nicest people that we'd ever want to meet."

"Doubtful, and I believe you know that. We've been hearing about the Savages all our lives and know the stories like they're our own. Remember the stories about Helen and Mercury? She thought the world revolved around them?" Tank knew that to be right, but didn't agree with his brother. "There are others, too. Their kids are more than likely the same way. You've heard the saying as much as I have, the apple doesn't fall far from the tree."

"I know what you're saying, but wouldn't it be nice to have some family around once in a while? Especially during the holidays?" The holidays were quite boring if you asked him. Once the holidays were over, it was as if they'd never been celebrated in their homes. Even the Christmas tree—if they bothered to put one up, was taken down the day after Christmas and put away until about ten days before it came around again. "Maybe it won't be all fun and games with them, but I'd like to know that we tried a little bit to get to know them."

"There might not be any reason for us to get worked up about them. They may get the notification and toss it out like you should have done when it came in the mail." Tank decided that his brother might be right and told him that. "I'm always right. When are you going to get that in your head, little brother?"

They laughed, then hugged. They'd only had each other their entire lives. They'd of course had their parents, but they were neither close as children nor as adults. As they got older, they realized that their parents had eyes only for each other and not for them. He supposed they were loved in a fashion, but nothing earthshattering. Even now, they had very little to do with them unless it was something that they needed from them, and even then, it was as a last-ditch effort to contact them.

Ace was the older of the two of them by ten days. When they were kids, he used to lord it over him like it was ten years rather than a few days. As they got older, it didn't seem to matter much to either of them because they, again, were all they had. He supposed it was best that they were alone now, as they were pursuing things that their parents wouldn't approve of. But they needed money, and that was the only way of getting any was to have a job. And with their magic, being a PI was the best kind of way to make money.

Tank could trace people that he'd had contact with. A small touch meant that he could find you no matter where you ended up hiding. Be it another country or even hidden deep into the ground in a shelter of some sort. He'd be able to find you. Ace had the bigger magic.

He could trace phone calls, no matter how many times you had it bounce off another server; he could easily hit all of the places you'd set up to block him, and he'd still be able to trace a person. Even computers were no match for him. Text messages were easier than phone calls, but he would trace them back to the source without any issues. Bondsmen had been using him to find people who would skip out on their bail for years now, and they loved him for it. So he decided that being a PI would net them more money and bigger jobs to find people.

Neither of them could find an object through their magic. He supposed that they hadn't really tried to make that work for them. They both often wondered if they would get more magic if they were to meet their mates. Something that neither of them was opposed to but didn't think would ever happen. They weren't wealthy by any stretch of the imagination; they had magic, but for the most part, it wasn't very good. Neither one could drive. They couldn't afford a car, so why bother with keeping up with a license was their motto.

"We have our first client." As they went over the notes that Ace had taken from the man, he wasn't at all surprised to find that the man was human. Humans didn't trust one another, and it showed in the way that they worked at their relationships with one another. Not even married couples were trustful of each other. Not like mates for shifters anyway. "He believes that his wife is cheating on him, and he wants us to find the truth. I'm going to go to the club where she works and get in contact with her. It might just be that he's a jealous type and she's younger than him, but I doubt it. I'll go there now."

While his brother was gone, he set up the file for the case. They were going to number everything that went with the case the same number, so there wasn't any confusion as to what was going on. As soon as his brother came back, they'd start on the case and have it worked up in a few short hours. It was something that they prided their selves on and that was getting cases closed up quickly.

It seemed to be taking his brother forever to return to the house they rented. He reached out to him once and was told to stop until he contacted him. He sounded so serious that he knew something had happened at the club that the woman hung out at when her husband was working. It was nearly midnight when Ace finally got back to him.

"She's dead. The woman that I went to see is dead, and her husband killed her. He hired us, then went to the club to tell her what he'd done and pulled out a knife and slit her throat. Just like that." Tank asked what she'd been doing. *"The client said she was sitting on the lap of one of the patrons, but I don't know about that. When I got here, she was sitting at the bar alone and doing nothing to attract anyone to her."*

"Did you tell the police that?" Ace told him that everyone had told them that. *"But he killed her anyway. Why did he bother hiring us if all he was going to do was kill her right afterwards?"*

"I have an idea he was hoping that we'd find something, but when he went to the club and found her alone, he was so pissed off that he killed her right then and there. The police are saying that it was premeditated because he brought the knife with him." Ace asked him to hang on a moment while he spoke to the police. *"I'll get back with you at home. I don't know what happens now."*

It took another three hours before his brother came home. And another two hours to go over everything that he'd seen at the place. The client had been arrested, of course, and the police knew that they had been hired. That was the reason he'd given for being at the club. It was scary to him the lengths humans would go to in order to have things go their way. He wanted her to be having an affair and was pissed off that she wasn't doing what he wanted for the divorce he was sure to get if it could be proven. Humans were off their rockers, he thought to himself.

The next morning, the police came by to question Ace again. He'd been sitting close to the woman when she'd been killed, and the police had just wanted to clear things up before the case went to court. The deposit that the client had put down on the work they were to have done for him was completed, they told them, and the money was theirs to keep. He hoped that would be what happened as the case was going nowhere now. The thousand dollars would go a long way in keeping the electricity on, as well as food in the house.

Tank was sitting at the desk, filling out the last of the case file, when the phone rang. He nearly didn't answer it for fear it was going to be about the case again. But as soon as he picked it up, a tingling went down his arm and to his chest. The man at the other end was someone that he never thought to speak to, even though he'd told Ace that they could call them.

"This is Tucker Savage. We got a notification that we're related from the DNA tests we sent in to the company called *Relationships*. The company didn't give us any names, but as I said, I'm Tucker of the Savage family." Tank told him that he was called Tank, but his real name was Sherman Savage. "You must resemble a tank, then? I'm not sure about that, but I can see you as a linebacker for a football team."

"I'm built like a Tank, yes. And I did play some ball in high school and college. Right up until I blew out my knee when I was a senior. We didn't get names either, with the results only showing that we were related to you guys. You're part of the Mercury and Helen Savage family, isn't that right? That's where we come in. We're the sons of

Mildred and Hank Savage. My father was the half-brother of Mercury." He asked if they wanted to get together. "I would love that, as will my brother. My parents aren't going to be a part of this reunion of sorts, as they wanted nothing to do with the family after we were born. I don't know what happened, but I can tell you that we're unable to shift, but we do have magic."

They talked for an hour or so before Tucker asked if they could set up a meeting where they got to know all of the cousins. He was excited to learn that they were nice-sounding dragons and that Helen and Mercury had been taken care of by the council. He wasn't sure what that might have entailed, but if the counsel was involved, it had to have been serious. He and Ace had said that they wanted nothing to do with the older dragons if they could help it, and were glad that the cousins sounded just as nice as they could be.

"You do know that it could be a scam, don't you? For all we know, they're the same, if not worse than Helen was all our lives. As I've said before, you've heard the stories as much as I have." He said that he knew that when he was telling Ace that Tucker had called. "I don't know that I'd trust them to follow through on sending a car for us either. Nor the plane ticket to get to see them. I know I've said this a dozen times to you, but please don't get your hopes up only to have them dashed when things don't work out."

"I'm trying. Tucker is married to a woman by the name of Kaida, she's human, and Kingston, he goes by Kings, is mated to a woman by the name of Skye, also a human, and they have a son named Trevor." Ace was impressed that they shared that much information. "He seemed really nice. There were times when I was talking to him that I felt like he was genuine and friendly. I don't know that he's any happier with his lot in life with his family than we have been. I also told him that our parents wanted nothing to do with them. He seemed all right with that as well."

"When are we supposed to go there? You know we have our new business starting up, so we can't just drop everything and go." Tank said he wasn't worried about the business, that things would work out with it. "Did you tell them what sort of jobs we had? I mean, did it come up that we're dirt poor?"

"No. I have a feeling that he has money, though. I don't know about the other four cousins, but he just sounded like he didn't have the daily worry that we did." He asked him what he meant. "He said they owned a couple of houses that we could stay in as they were furnished and that we could stay for as long as we liked. They would love to get to know us."

"Maybe they'll see that we're the poor end of the family and decide to send us back home with our tail between our legs." Tank asked his brother when he'd gotten so negative all the time. "I don't know that I'm that way all the time, but in this, I think that I'm right in saying that they're going to be disappointed in us when they meet us. And I don't care if they want to get to know us, I'm going to come back here and live the life that we've carved out for ourselves, regardless of how much we have in common with them."

"I agree." His agreement seemed to shock his

brother, so he explained. "That's why I'm saying it will matter little if we leave the business for a few days. We can get messages on the phone and work from anywhere, and if they don't like us, we can just do as you said. Come back home and just live our lives like we'd been doing, but be a little wiser about family matters."

The car was going to take them to the airport on Friday morning and then bring them back from it on Tuesday afternoon. They would be flying there; it was going to be a short trip from North Carolina, and they were looking forward to the trip now that they'd come to the conclusion that things with the other side of their family didn't matter all that much. They'd take it one day at a time, and that was all they were going to hope for.

They had three days to get their things gathered up that they were going to pack. It wasn't going to be a great deal of packing as both of them could change their clothes with a thought. They could also feed themselves thanks to Ace's magic, and so all they worried about was having a carry-on so they had some kind of luggage when they got to the airport. He was taking his laptop so that he had something to work with. And Ace was taking his cell phone that was paired with the phone in the office that they used. Things were going to work out for them no matter what kind of people their newfound relatives were.

The morning of the ride to the airport was a beautiful day. Most people would say that every day was beautiful in North Carolina, but they had seen their homes destroyed by all kinds of weather. That was all they had: the rental that they used for the business and their home that they'd gotten from their parents when they moved more inland along the coast. He supposed they could sell it for a great deal of money, but they wouldn't have the ocean views that they had now. It was a win-win for them, he thought.

The tickets were at the airport for them to use. Both of them had been excited that they were in first class on the plane and couldn't believe how much room they had while sitting up front. There wasn't a meal or anything; the trip wasn't all that long, but there had been drinks and snacks that they partook of and were happy that they had come this far at least. Tank was happy to see that his brother seemed to be in a better mood about getting together with their relatives, and it made him less stressed about it as well.

They were met at the airport in Zanesville by the family. It had surprised him that they had all taken time out of their day to come to greet them. Then, after they had gotten together to go to dinner, they had a wonderful time getting to know them, and he was especially happy that they didn't seem bothered by their lack of dragons either.

Since it was so late when they arrived after dinner, they were taken to the home they were going to be using while visiting. The house was fully staffed, which they hadn't expected, and it was done up nicely for them. They each had their own rooms, and it was an ensuite room, so that they didn't even have to share a bathroom. If this was what money could buy a person, he thought that he could get used to it fairly quickly and never turn back to being poor.

~*~

Kings like the two younger men. They were smart and savvy and seemed to have a good head on their shoulders. Since Tucker had gotten to know Tank the best, it was fun to get to know both men as they seemed to have different personalities but similar in a way that made you realize that they were related. They certainly didn't look all that much alike.

"We've been trying our best to just live out our lives while trying to figure out what to do with ourselves. The PI business has come as both a blessing and a terror." Ace told him about the happenings at the club on their first assignment. "She was a beautiful woman, and to have had her throat cut like that surely was a shame for her family too. She'll be greatly missed. Her husband is in jail now for his part in her death."

"We've had some things going on around here as well." Kings told Ace about how his mate and the boy that she'd been protecting had come to be a part of their family. "They're still in jail, but I know that the judge will be hearing pretrial information in the coming weeks. Right now, he's got all he needs to tell if there is going to be a trial or not, but I don't see that being an issue. They both have murdered people, and there is proof of them doing it. In fact, Waggoner has confessed to murdering a lot of people and seems to take pride in his work."

"I can help you if you'd like us to get involved with it. Tank and I have enough magic that we never have to do anything more than to touch the people that we're working with. One of us should be able to trace back to all the people who have been killed, and that would surely help in keeping them in jail. Where it sounds like they need to be."

"That would be fantastic." They talked a bit more about how their magic worked, and as soon as they could set it up, one of them would go to the jail and see the other three, and that would be all it would take to keep them behind bars. "Maybe then my wife will stop having nightmares about Waggoner. She doesn't have them nightly, but they bother her enough that she's terrified some nights."

"It would be my pleasure to help her out with that. I've never had a nightmare, but I've heard enough about them that it makes me think that I'm lucky that I've not." Kings told him that he'd never had one either, but he knew firsthand what it could do to someone who was in the middle of them. "I bet it makes you feel helpless. I know that it would me if my mate was having dreams that I couldn't do anything about."

Kings kept an eye on the two men and his mate. Skye seemed to be enjoying their company, but he wasn't sure about Trevor. While not really an outgoing young man, he did seem to be keeping his distance from him and was going to figure out why as soon as possible. It might be nothing more than they were strangers and that was it, but he wouldn't know until he talked to the younger man.

When Ace got a phone call, he stepped outside to take it. He hoped it was a job for the two men as they seemed desperate to make their PI business a success. When Ace came back and went to his brother, he figured it was going to be a job and wished in some way that he could help them. But he knew nothing about the job of being a PI and even less about the two cousins he now had.

Kings drove them home after the dinner and told them if they wanted to change anything, just do it. They didn't have to ask for permission, he told them, as he wanted them to be comfortable when they were here and there was little to nothing that they wouldn't approve of anyway. They just wanted them to be comfortable during their stay. After dropping them off, he made his way home with his own family, but didn't get the opportunity to ask Trevor about his behavior when talking to the other two.

"I was wondering something. And you can tell me it's none of my business if you want. But why haven't you slept in the master bedroom when it's clearly where you should be?" He told her that he actually liked the bedroom that he was in more and hoped that sometime he could convince her to make it the master suite instead of the one that she was currently using. "I'd have to see it, but this is your house. You can do whatever you want, and no one would say anything."

"I had hopes that someday I'd be sharing the room with you, and I want you to be happy. The room has a better view, and if you come with me now, we can see the deer that are usually out this time of day." She said that she'd love that. "I was hoping to bring you down to the room sooner rather than later, so this is perfect timing."

The family of deer was out, and it looked as if sometime over the last couple of days they'd given birth to two little fawns. They were covered in spots and seemed to be having fun being out in the open with their parents. The buck wasn't that old either; his horns were just beginning to look large, and the mother seemed to be a good one as she kept an eye on the two little ones as they romped around the yard.

"I was wondering something. When are we going to have sex?" He didn't have an answer, so he just looked at her. "I know you said nothing would happen unless I wanted it to, so I'm wondering what I have to do to tell you that I'm ready?"

"You could just say I'm ready to make love with you, and that would work. Or you could just meet me in my bed one night and I'd be more than willing to oblige you." She asked him which would be better for him. "Since we're going to make love this first time in the bedroom, I'd say that you're in the perfect place to make that happen."

"I want to have sex with you. However, there are a couple of things that you should know about me. I've had sex before. It was good, but nothing that I'd want to again. However, I think it'll be different with you. You'd be...consuming to me, I think is the correct wording." He didn't have a comment for her about him consuming her, so he asked her what else he needed to know. "I've fallen in love with you. I know that it's quick, but I think that four or five months is a good amount of time to see what sort of person you are. And you seem like a reasonable man. You don't cut at me anymore. You're also very good to Trevor, which is the number one reason for me to fall in love with you."

"I love you as well. I think that I have since I first met you. Even though I tried to be a good man, you make me want to be a better one." She seemed satisfied with his answer and turned to watch the deer again. "Are we making love tonight? Or is this just to build up until the time that we do?"

"I'd very much like to make love in this room. You're right about it being a better room. I enjoy the windows that are in here as well as the shape of this room. While I've not been in the bed, it looks bigger than the one that I'm currently sleeping in, and that's good since we'll be sharing it. I do have one request. If I have a nightmare, don't think it's because of you. I have them regularly now."

"I know that. I can hear you every time you have one. I only want to break down your door once or twice a week to comfort you. Perhaps us sleeping together will make you feel safe from Waggoner, and you won't have them anymore." She said that would thrill her to no end, not having nightmares anymore. "Good. Then I'll make it my priority to make sure you feel as safe as I can make you while we're sleeping together. Is there anything else I should know?"

"Yes." She didn't go any further with her answer, and he wondered at that. After watching the deer a bit more, she turned to him and smiled as she wrapped her arms around his shoulders. "I'm not afraid of you like I think I should be. However, I wish to see your dragon. I saw Tucker's the other day when he was with Kaida. He's red and beautiful. I don't think that yours will be any less beautiful, but I'd like to see him as soon as you can manage it."

"All right. In the morning. I show you and Trevor both. He's been asking to see him as well." She nodded and leaned into his body. "I want you with every fiber of my being, and I'll be as gentle with you as you allow me to be."

Leaning down, he kissed her on the mouth and made love to it with his tongue. She seemed hesitant at first, but then enjoyed the play between them as well. Picking her up, he took her to the bed for the first time. He wanted it to be perfect for the two of them and was glad that they'd gotten to know one another better before having sex.

Chapter 4

Skye wasn't kidding Kings when she told him that sex hadn't meant anything to her before. It seemed more like a duty to her after several dates with the same person that she gave in. While she had enjoyed it to a degree, she never felt the satisfaction of it, nor did she feel what some people described as earth-shattering. The bed hadn't even moved for her, much less the entire world.

It was going to be different with Kings, she'd thought. He'd be consuming to her. While she knew what the word meant, she wasn't entirely sure why it was the first word that came to her when she thought about having sex with the big man. And lord, he was big.

His shoulders were broad enough that she thought that she could sit on him and he'd not notice the extra weight. Not that she was all that big herself, but she liked to think she could hold her own when it came to making love or just having plain sex with someone that she wanted in her bed. When he laid her on the big bed, she drew in a deep breath and could have sworn that she could smell herself. Embarrassed now that they were going to be having sex, she tried stirring around on the bed to hide the smell.

"You're only making it more prevalent. I have smelled you since we entered this room." She said she didn't know what was wrong with her. "You're aroused.

Your heat is calling to me. There is something else you should know. If we have sex right now, you're going to be carrying our child. If that's something that you don't want to happen right now, tell me and I'll take precautions."

"I don't know what you mean. I'm on the pill and I have been for years. It was the one thing that I made sure I could afford all the time I was running from Jason." He explained to her how it wouldn't matter, as he was stronger than anything man-made when it came to birth control. "Then how will you take precautions? Would you wear a condom?"

"No, I wouldn't enter you until you're no longer in season. Or in heat, whatever you wish to call it." She thought about what he was saying, and then she thought of carrying his child. It was something that she'd given a great deal of thought about, but nothing so soon. "It's entirely up to you, love. I will abide by your wishes on any decision you make. It's your body, and I would never do anything like this without making sure you've thought about it completely."

"I want to have your child someday, but I never thought of it being so soon." He nodded as if she'd given him the decision that she'd wanted. "However, the thought of being large with your child makes me love you all the more. I would love to have your child. I know very little about rearing a dragon child, but I'll be the best at it as I can be with you beside me when we do have one."

"I love you." She told him that she loved him as well and told him that she was ready. "As am I, my love."

He stood up next to the bed, and she sat on the edge. It seemed silly to her that she was shy about showing him her body and her seeing his, but they'd come this far and she was going to see it through. Once he had his shirt off and it was tossed to the floor, she knew a renewed need for him that she'd never felt before. He seemed to understand her, too.

"You're larger than I could see in your shirts." He said that he wore them larger so as not to frighten her. "Thank you for that. It's good to know that you've been protecting me even after all this time."

She stood up, and he took a step back. Unbuttoning her blouse seemed to be giving her fits because she was distracted by each part of his wonderful body he exposed when he took something else off. Even when he loosened up his belt and tossed it away, she felt herself getting wetter with each breath she took.

With his pants open and his shoes off, she reached down to touch the skin from where he had unbuttoned his pants. The tip of his cock barely touched her, but she drew in a sharp breath; he was larger than she'd realized again, and thought that making love with him would be...well, it would be painful.

"I won't hurt you." She nodded, not really believing that it would be possible. "I promise you that I will make it easier for you than you think possible at the moment. Lean back on the bed and let me have a look at the wonders of your body."

"I'm not all that much to look at. My breasts are too small, and I have large hips. Birthing hips is what my grandmother said of them." She watched as he helped her lie back on the bed and then get down on his knees. Again, it made her wet, and she wasn't as embarrassed about it as she had been before. "You're so handsome, Kings. How did you manage to be single just when I came along?"

"I've been waiting for you my entire life." He pulled her panties off under her skirt and then reached up and pulled her skirt off. "I've been wanting you this way for a while now."

Running his hands up her legs to her thighs, she could feel his breath on her body. It was hot, hotter than it would have normally been, and she wanted to feel it all over herself. When he lifted her legs up and put them over his shoulders, she tried to close herself off to him, but it did little good. He could see all of her, and she was beginning to feel like he was going to give her everything that she could have hoped for in the form of sex.

"I'm going to eat you." She let out a long held breath and told him good. "That's my girl. I'm going to taste you as long as you'll allow me to. Then I'm going to fuck you until you come apart in my arms. Would you like that?"

"Yes. Oh please. Give yourself to me." Leaning down to her pussy he blew his breath over her curls. She knew that they were wet, and the warm air blown over them made her want more of him. As soon as he touched her with his mouth, his tongue touching her clit, she came apart with a scream that she could barely hold onto behind her teeth. "More. Please, I need more."

He spread her nether lips with his hands over her thighs, and she cried out when he put his mouth over her. When his tongue played with her clit, she rode his mouth like she was riding him. Hard and fast movements that served only in making her want more of him. He was making her crazy by sucking on her then fucking her with his tongue. Nothing could have prepared her for the way it felt to be made love to this way.

As she rode his mouth, she played with her breasts. They seemed to be very sensitive right now, and she wanted the feeling to be everywhere on her body. As she pinched her nipples and rolled them with her fingers, she felt her pussy gush out some more of the cream that she was leaking down her thighs.

Skye lost count of the number of times that she came. Her head was spinning, and her body felt heavy. When Kings slid his fingers into her, she came up off the bed with a scream, knowing that she had climaxed several times in a row, and it made her dizzy with need. He was going to kill her; she just knew it.

Her body had been through so much in the last several minutes. All she could think about was how much more she could take, knowing on some level that he knew what he was doing, and the next time she hit that point, she wasn't going to be able to contain herself and reached down to hold onto to Kings as he continued to fuck her with his fingers.

"More. I need more." He hummed a little, and she cried out. It didn't seem to matter that she was wrung out from his lovemaking; there was more to be had, and she wanted it from him now. Grabbing his hair, she pulled him from her and looked down her body at him. "Christ."

His face was covered in her cream. His lips were swollen, and his cheeks were a dusty rose color. The grin he had on his face reminded her of what a child would look like who'd been given a treat that would last them all day. Her heart pounded in her chest with the love that she had for him, and it was all she could do to not allow him to continue with the pleasure torture that he was tormenting her body with.

"Fuck Skye, you're beautiful right now." Nodding, unsure what to say to him, she begged him to fuck her. "All right, soon. I love you so much."

Instead of putting her off like she thought that he might, he stood up, and she could see his cock had leaked all over the front of his boxer briefs. She wondered for a moment how many times he'd come like he was, and then he stripped off his underwear and tossed them to the side. He stood before her in all his glory and wonderment.

His body was perfect in shape and size. His chest was as large as she'd seen before, but it was the tuft of hair that covered his nipples down to his groin and the cock that was standing straight out from his root. He was larger than she'd ever had before, but she was no longer worried about him hurting her. She knew that he'd done as he said and prepared her for his cock as much as he could.

Moving her to the middle of the bed so that her feet were no longer dangling off the side, he made his way up her body, kissing parts of her that he passed. First her ankles, then her calves. As he lingered on her knees, she dug her nails into the mattress to hang on to it. Whatever happened, she knew she was going to come apart, and she wanted to hold onto something so she'd come back down on the bed.

Then he kissed her hip bone, her ribs. As he suckled at her breasts, Skye held them to his mouth. She could feel his cock against her thigh and moaned from the heat of it. As he moved up her more, stopping at her chin, then her throat to snuggle her there, she released the bed to hold him to her. As he lifted his head from her throat, she watched his face as he held his cock to enter her.

He entered her slowly and gently. When his cock seemed to be too large for her, he fucked her, slightly moving his cock deeper within her as he did so. When he was fully seated inside of her, she wrapped her ankles around his hips and let him stay there. She could tell that he was straining not to hurt her, and she couldn't have loved him anymore for being so kind to her.

"Take me." He nodded but didn't move. "I want to feel you inside of me, Kingston. Please give me all that you are."

"I don't want to hurt you, but it's killing me right now." She moved her own hips and felt herself stretch for him. Rocking upward into his cock, she could feel the moment that he was fully inside of her, and she felt like she could feel his cock at the back of her throat. "Oh, baby, yes."

She was nearly blinded by him taking her. When he put his hand under her hip and pulled her up to meet his downward strokes, she cried out again as the pleasure overrode any pain. Once he took her mouth, she knew she was going to come when her entire body seemed to have frozen in place seconds before she passed out from the head-rolling climax that took her breath away.

Not being out for very long, she held onto Kings as he took her higher and higher. Once he started fucking her hard, not holding back at all, it was all she could do to keep up with him. Watching his face as he stared into her eyes, she caught the moment that he was coming a split second before she felt the first splash of cum filling her sheath as he took her even higher, and she simply fell over the edge.

It started out softly, like she was rolling through a nice summer storm. Her body felt it coming as they connected on some other level. As soon as she began her descent into bright colors that were behind her eyelids, she held tighter onto Kings as she cried out over and over that she was coming with him. Then, like a snap of a rubber band on your wrist, she was out again.

~*~

Kings was worn out. Not only had he come harder than he'd ever come in his life, but his heart was still pounding, and his body felt electrified by every breath she breathed across his body and every time her body adjusted to his. Finally, when it became too much, he rolled over, taking her body with him as he lay on his back.

He knew on some level that he'd not killed his pretty mate, but he found himself checking on her often. Adjusting her body so that she lay beside him, he made sure that she was covered up with the blankets as the room had chilled enough that he could feel it. Watching her sleep or being passed out, he wasn't sure which, he thought that she was the most beautiful creature he'd ever encountered. And she was going to have his child.

Putting his hand over her still flat belly, he leaned over to kiss her there. When Skye's fingers tangled in his hair, he looked up at her and smiled. She was awake now, and he wanted to tell her how much more he'd fallen in love with her.

"I love you too. I've never felt like this after sex.

Thank goodness. I might well have made a career out of it if it had ever been this good." He told her she belonged to him. "I know that. I know that more than ever now."

They talked about nothing at all. Just whatever subject came to them. Once he could no longer hide that he was starving, he got up, dressed himself, and headed to the kitchen. Before leaving her, however, he started a bath for her so that she could clean up before they enjoyed the hot tub together. He'd been using it nightly since it had been delivered the week before.

Getting things out of the fridge, he was excited to find that sandwiches had been made by the cook and put on a platter. Leaving behind a few of them so that Trevor could find them, he took that as well as a bag of chips — his favorite snack up to their bedroom with a bottle of wine and two glasses. Skye was just getting out of the tub when he arrived back in the room.

The hot tub was a big one; it could hold up to six people, but it was perfect for the two of them. Once he put the sandwiches on the side table and poured them some wine, he was ready to make love to Skye again, but she winced when moving around in the warm water.

"I think I might have broken something important." He laughed, knowing that until he got back in the room, he was feeling a little broken himself. "I think that's the first time in my life I've ever fainted. Especially during sex."

"You scared me a little when you did, and now that you're fully awake, I can tell you that I checked your breathing several times while I lay there with you." She laughed as he had hoped that she would. "I feel like a new man."

"I feel sort of strange." He was hurt, but before he could ask her what she meant, she spoke again. "Right now, my body feels like it's tingling all over. Is that normal?"

"Magic." He'd forgotten that she might get more magic from him and would be creating her own. "Honey, I'm going to pick you up and put you to bed."

Before he could get her out of the hot tub, she was stiffening up. He could see the pain on her face; her eyes were glazed over with it. Before he was able to lie her down, he could feel his own body tingling and thought that she'd said it right. It felt like from his toes to his head, his body was beginning to tingle and make him aware that he'd just bonded with his mate.

The pain for her had her screaming about it. His own pain was bad, but he was able to hold onto Skye as her body writhed in pain. Even as she begged him to stop the pain, his own was getting out of control. The last thing that he remembered seeing was Tucker there holding his hand as the pain finally consumed him. His only hope was that Skye was all right and wasn't dying like he felt like he was.

Opening his eyes, he didn't move, not even to blink. But he could see that someone was in the room with him, and there was a weight in the bed that he thought was Skye, but that's as far as his ability to reason out what had happened to him went.

"Before you ask, Skye is still resting. I tried to put the two of you in separate beds, the way you were writhing around, but you wouldn't have her gone from you. Finally, we just let the two of you wrestle it out for yourselves." He had to clear his throat twice before he could ask how long they'd been out. "Four days. I will tell you that I was worried about the two of you for being out for so long, but my little dragon said you were fine, and I had to believe her. Are you well?" He'd forgotten that Tucker called his mate his little dragon. It was what her name meant, Little Dragon.

"I'm still taking inventory of myself." Tucker laughed, and so did he, but he stopped when it hurt. "I'm assuming that you've been here the whole time."

"I was afraid to leave you two. You were really in a great deal of pain even after the large tremors you were having stopped." He nodded, not feeling as much pain as he'd felt when he had laughed. "You've had visitors since you've been resting. Mostly, it was the cousins; they were concerned for you when they felt it like I had that the two of you had bonded. The others felt it too."

"What do you mean, felt it?" He was able to sit up now and was glad that he had on some sweatpants. Looking at Skye, she was dressed in the shirt that he wore with the pants he had on. "Someone dressed us."

"No, you were dressed like you are now when I came here. I didn't know what had happened, so I broke down the door. I've since had it replaced." Thanking him, he continued to stare at Skye. "She's been moaning in her sleep. I thought that she was having nightmares, but you started doing the same thing, and I just figured it was because you'd bonded. Do you have any idea why most of the dragons that I know felt that you two bonded? I have an idea, but nothing concrete."

"I've only just figured out that I'm not dead or dismembered. Tell me what you think happened, and I'll give that some thought." He told him. "I don't think that's even remotely true, do you? Why would I be the leader of our group of dragons? I mean, I've never even had that thought enter my mind at being in charge."

"There could be another reason for it, and I'm not sure you're going to like that one any better than you did my theory about you being in charge of us all." He asked him what it was. "That you and Skye are more powerful than any other dragon we know, and a lot we don't know. That would also lead me back to you being in charge, but you said that wasn't possible, so I have no idea. Oh, yeah, there is another thing. Faeries showed up about the time I got here. They've been running your house for you. I've not bothered to talk to them; they seemed to know what they're here for."

"Faeries? I've not seen faeries since I was about twenty and they came around to talk to me." He asked if he had. "No, my mother forbid it. Said I was nothing that would warrant faeries coming around, and she told them to go away. That would have been the day that I was able to shift for the first time."

"You do realize that isn't making your case for not being in charge any less true." Washing his hands over his face, he looked at his long-time friend. "You've this incredible power, I can almost see it on you, and you've been out for four days just adjusting to it. Or it could have been the sex. I wasn't here, so I have no idea. Anyway, you have faeries in your house — and not a few either, but I'd say a couple of pips."

"Remind me what a pip is?" He told him. "You think that I have two large groups of faeries in my house right now? That's not possible. I mean, the house is big enough, but why would there be that many faeries in my household?"

"Why are you using so many words this early in the morning?" They both turned to look at Skye. She had covered her head with the sheet, and he had to laugh. "Who are you talking to, and why are they in our bedroom? Tucker? Is that you? Why are you bothering us after we've had the most incredible sex in my life?"

"It's been four days, and I've been watching over you. Along with the others. Today was my turn." She sat up quickly and stared at Tucker. "Your mate and I were just discussing how much magic you guys got when you woke up."

"What do you mean by four days? There's no way that we've been out for...I mean, I feel kinda good about the rest, so perhaps. But you never mentioned being out for so long when you mentioned magic to me." Kings told her that they had a theory. "What sort of theory? Right now, my body is humming. Like it has too much energy in it and I'm going to explode."

"I feel it too. Like something has put us on a charger and we've hit the max." They both looked at Tucker when he laughed. "You're not the least bit funny, and whoever told you that you were was lying to you."

"I was just thinking again how much you're proving my point to be true." When Tucker stood up, so did he. "Give me a hug, big guy, and I'll be on my way. You have enough to contend with without me being here laughing at you all the time."

After he left them, Skye said she was going to take a shower. Before he could stop her or even to ask if she thought that was a good idea, the way they were feeling, she was gone to the bathroom. He stayed on the side of the bed, trying to figure out what he'd been told. But all he kept coming back to was that the faeries had wanted to talk to him when he'd first shifted into a dragon. Why would his mother forbid them? What had they wanted from him? He would have given it to them gladly; he knew that without the faeries, he'd be nothing. Getting up when there was a scratching sound at the door. He opened it to find several of the small creatures flying at his head level.

"Lord Savage? We've come to bring you something to eat." Moving out of the way of the horde that came into the room, he could smell the food even before they put it on a table that hadn't been there before. "Your cook will be adequate for the kitchen so long as we're there to make sure that the food is up to your standards."

"Standards? I don't understand what's going on. We usually have our breakfast in the kitchen with the cook." The one who had been doing the talking seemed to be put out. But he forged on. "Why are you guys even in my house? I don't remember anyone telling me who allowed you to take over in the first place."

"No one told us, your lordship." He corrected the faerie by telling him that he was just Kingston or Kings if he preferred. "Your lordship, we're here because you took a mate. We should have been with you all along, but your mother forbade us from having anything to do with you. Now that she's been imprisoned and no longer around to tell us what to do, we've come to make your life easier while at home and working."

"My life here at home was never in question. And what do you mean, no one is telling you what to do? This is my home, and I'll make the rules regarding you and the others." Skye came out of the bathroom and looked spitting mad. "Now look what you've done. You've upset my mate. And for what reason?"

"You are our king. She is our queen." He almost told the little creature that it wasn't possible, but something else occurred to him, and it was that they'd been called king and queen, not the lordship in charge of a small group of dragons like Tucker thought. "It's our duty to make sure that you are happy and well taken care of. We can do no less than that because of who you are."

"What makes you think that we even want to be king or queen?" That was an excellent question, and he was glad that Skye had asked it. "We have a good life as it is now without all this bothersome of faeries around all the time. Did you know that we can make our own way to the breakfast table without eating in our room? Also, this is our private place. You'll not be allowed to enter here unless one of us gives you permission to do so. If we keep you around at all. You're messing up our schedule."

Kings put his arms over his chest in a show that he agreed with everything that Skye had said. When the pip of them left the room, in a hurry, it seemed to him. He was faced with the one who had been seemingly in charge. His name wasn't as important right now since they were establishing who was in charge, and it wasn't going to be the tiny man with wings.

Ignoring the breakfast that had been brought up for them, he and Skye decided to go to the kitchen, where they had their first meal of the day every day. As soon as they were in the warm room, they could see the chaos of having a bunch of people in charge and no one doing a thing. It was Skye who took them to task and told them to go to another room so that they might enjoy their breakfast. Kings thought it was funny but wisely kept his laughter to a minimum.

Trevor joined them a few minutes after the pip left them to their meal. He didn't seem to notice anything going on, and they didn't tell him. But he had to have noticed the great amount of faeries that had been just in the other room when he came through, but he didn't say a word. He only asked for more pancakes when he finished what he had on his plate. The kid was going with the flow better than they were.

Chapter 5

It took hours to find out what was going on. After talking to the little people, her mind seemed not ready to believe that they were faeries, Skye had to call a meeting with the person in charge of sending them to their home, for her and Kings to get the total workout of why they were at the house and taking over.

"They weren't supposed to take over. I don't know why they would have." Skye told Lady Earth that she didn't either, as they had been just fine without them. "I understand what you're saying, but I believe they thought that they were to make sure that everything was just so for you and your mate."

"Just so, how? They invaded our bedroom, brought food into the room without our knowledge, and upset the cook into her thinking that she was going to be dismissed because she was only 'adequate'. There were at least a dozen more things they got into that weren't helpful at all. Including moving around the house to suit some kind of plan they had in their heads." She tsked at her. "What's that supposed to mean? You don't believe me?"

"No, it's not that at all. I just had no idea that Lord Kingston had never been informed of his new status as king of the dragons. It was my understanding that when he was just twenty-two, the pip in charge of his new status went there to talk to him and was supposed to be preparing him for his role as king centuries ago." Skye explained again what had happened. "I wasn't informed of that. I was only told that it had been taken care of and that they were working with him to get things in order. He should have been paid monthly for the role he was coming into."

"You're saying that he's been king since he shifted the first time?" Lady Earth said that was what her understanding of the situation had been. "They never spoke to him. His mother forbade it, as I have said twice now. He's had no contact with—who has been in charge all this time if it wasn't Kings?"

"No one, I can only assume. My goodness, this is a mess." She didn't bother telling her that it was a royal fuck up, but let her go on thinking it was simply a mess. "I'll have to go back and see what happened. The only reason that I can see now that they went to him is that I felt his taking of a mate. And I don't know how you feel about this, but it was a grand gesture for him to find you. And now that you're to have his child—I'm so sorry about all this. Someone screwed up badly." Again, she said nothing.

Not that she wanted to lash out at the other woman, but things like this, Kings falling through the cracks as it were, was something that should never have happened if someone was keeping up with the order of things. They should find the original person in charge and fire them at the very least.

After trying to find the faerie in charge, things went from bad to worse. He tried saying that he'd been watching over Kings since the day he'd been chosen, but couldn't recall anything that had happened in his adulthood to verify what he'd been doing. Even Kings had said he thought that he would have noticed a faerie hanging around him, as well as the other cousins.

When Lady Earth left her home to go and do some more research, Skye went to have lunch with Tank and Ace. They were quickly becoming a part of the family, like they'd been a part of it from their birth. She loved having them around.

"What are we having today?" Lunches with them had been fun for Kaida and her. They would meet up and have a wonderful time, then the men would get together for dinner, and she'd heard that it was a blast. Kings was certainly enjoying his time with the two new arrivals. "I'm going to have taco salad. My favorite meal of all time for lunch."

"I've been thinking about what you said about us moving up here to be closer. There isn't a lot that we'd have to do to move here, but some of it might cost us a bit." She said she'd help them get out of their lease if that's the problem. "We do have a lease on our house, but we actually purchased the building that we're going to be working from. We thought that if we were to have a lease, there might be a time when we lose it for reasons that we can't foresee, and that would be the best way of keeping up with where we want to work."

"That makes perfect sense." She agreed with Kaida. "We can help you with that as well. There are things that we can do to make sure you have a place here that you can work from as well. Tucker owns a few buildings in the downtown area of this town, and it wouldn't be hard for him to lease them out for you."

She knew that they had money; all of them didn't

seem to have to work if they didn't want to, but other things were going on that she knew a little about, like the income from the rentals that Kings had and the ones that were sitting empty. But she'd not offer them up for the men since Kaida had already done it. But she'd be there if it came to that.

"We have another job while we're here. We're to look for a missing adult. I didn't catch that he'd been gone for nearly six years until we said we'd work on it. I'm kind of excited to start on this one. They have to have someone looking for him because of the insurance money. They want to declare him dead so they can collect on it." Skye asked Ace if they had any leads. "We've already found him. I have to be honest when I tell you that I'm surprised that they hired us. They've done nothing so far to prove or disprove that the man is anything but living. But they paid upfront, and that's mostly why we're doing this for the money. And he's not that far from here either. Just a few miles from his son's home, the person who hired us. You'd think that in all that time they would have come across each other at some point, wouldn't you?"

"I would have thought so. But then I don't go into town all that often and look for people that I might know." She shivered a little. "Gives me the creeps a little, to be honest. Why was he hiding out so close to his family and not contacting them? I'd have to figure that out too. Like, do they even want him found, or do they want to just declare him dead for the money?"

"I never thought of that when we found him. He doesn't seem to be taking any kind of precautions for where he's living in order not to be found. Perhaps he's not really missing and is rather pissed off at the family and wants them to leave him alone. Like you said, they didn't hire anyone but us in all this time." Kaida said she'd just tell them where he was and have nothing more to do with it.

"That way, if something happens like it did with the man and his wife, you won't be questioned about your part in it all. I don't want anything to happen to you two. I've grown quite fond of you over the last few weeks." They'd been together every evening since they arrived and had even been aware of her and Kings' bonding. In the month since they'd been there, they'd spent a great deal of time with them and had really gotten to know them quite well. "When are you going to tell them where he is?"

"Tomorrow. They're coming by the courthouse to get what information we have. I thought that it was the best place to meet with them as we didn't want to do anything without witnesses." Kaida said she'd be there, too, in the event that they needed backup. "That's very nice of you, but we don't want anything to happen to you guys either. You're the best family we've ever had."

"That's so sweet." It was, too. She'd been on the run with Trevor for years before they came to be a part of the Savage family, and she, like Ace and Tank, thought that they were coming out on the better end of the family with them in their lives. "Let's eat before we start crying like children."

Lunch was fun, and she really enjoyed her taco salad. It was something that filled her up, but it never made her feel overly heavy. Just as she was getting out her purse to pay for her food, Kaida said that she had all their meals and would pay for them. That was an unexpected bonus, one that she rather loved.

After lunch, she had two meetings to go to. Inviting the others to go with her, she knew that they'd be finished up in record time. One of the meetings was with the mayor and his plans for the school district's upcoming calendar. Which she had no idea why anyone would think that she had any say in the thing. Then they were meeting about the pool and the need for a lift to be put in for the people with disabilities who wanted to enjoy the pool as well.

Knowing that the men had already spoken with them about it didn't make her want to go to the meeting any better, but she would go so that she could tell them again that they would pay one-half of the bill to have it put in, and that was all. If they couldn't raise the other half, then it wasn't going to be on them. While they could all afford to put in the lift on their own, they decided that the town had its hands out a little too often now. They would like to curb their thinking that they were going to be given money for every project.

No one could figure out why she was there either, so she didn't stay long. After the meeting for the pool was called to order, she pulled out her notes on the last time they'd gotten together about this very thing. After reading over what was said, she told them that the Savages position hadn't changed, and if they wanted to get that put in, they'd have to raise part of the money.

"But it has to be put in. We're being fined daily for not even starting on the project." Kaida asked the mayor what the holdup was. "We can't afford another fundraiser this time of year. People are getting ready for back to school, and there's just no money set aside for something like this."

"I don't know what to tell you then. You've had two years to raise the money or not, and it's small wonder that you're getting fined. You were to start on this when it was brought up, and now that they're fining you, you decide that you can't afford to work on the project. That sounds like something you should have taken care of over the planters that you had filled for the sidewalks."

"That was from the beautification of the town money. Not the pool fund money." She said she didn't care where the money came from, but they were only going to fine them for so long before they started taking legal action. "You've had two years. Something should have been started by now."

"Why don't you just pay for it, and when times are better, we can pay you back for some of it?" She stood up with her notes and was ready to leave. This was the exact reason that the dragons had left their other town was that the town was forever in their pockets. She was nearly to the door when the mayor realized that she was really leaving the meeting. "You can't just walk out of here. We've not gotten anything finished or set up."

"As far as I'm concerned, the meeting is over. You've been told what the Savages would do, and you decided that wasn't enough. How about if we stop helping with projects all over the town?" The mayor, she really wished she knew what his name was, said that he'd sue them if they did that. "Good luck with that. We've been helping long enough. I believe that I can speak for the rest of us when I say good luck with the projects that you have on the list of things we were going to help you with."

She was out the door before she let him say another word. As soon as she was outdoors, she leaned against the building she had been in and covered her mouth before she felt like she was going to be sick. She hated confrontation, and this had been a huge one. Skye could only hope that the men of the family weren't upset with her when they found out that she'd stopped all projects in the city that were going on.

There were only two, but in order to make this stick, she made her way to the first project and halted work. Telling the supervisor that the Savages were no longer going to fund their part in the Works Department, and their new furnace and air conditioner being put in. The Works Department was the one in charge of the beautification projects around town. They had agreed to fund half the work when it was apparent that the building had no furnace or air conditioner that functioned. And with winter fast approaching, they'd need to have it fixed soon.

The second project that they'd been a part of was the expansion of the grocery store. It had burned down a few years ago, and they'd been able to get funding for it to be rebuilt. But it was much too small for their growing town, and they asked for money to double its size. She had them stop the work as well, and she was happy to see that they seemed to think it was funny that she was the one making them stop when the mayor had only yesterday told them to hurry up and get it finished, as he had more projects to work on. She reached out to Kings and told him what she'd done.

"*Brilliant. It should have been done years ago. Thank you for helping us out of that black hole.*" She told him that she thought that he'd be upset with her. "*For taking a stand against a bully? Never. He's just lucky I didn't go with you. I might well have shifted to my dragon and taken the place out. Then where would he be if the building had burnt to the ground? Moron. I'm happy you did it as well, the rest of the cousins will be when I tell them.*"

"*He wanted you to fund the pool project for the lift, and they'd pay you back when they had the money. I had a feeling that they'd never have the money for the project while others are going on. This wouldn't have been the end of it either, I don't think.*" He told her that he believed she was correct in that as well. "*I have nothing else to do today but to hang out with Ace and Tank. They're thinking of moving here, isn't that great?*"

"*It is. I hope they do. There is nothing like having a lot of family around that you like and having fun. Why don't we have them over for a cookout tonight? That was where you left off in convincing them; the rest of us can take over.*" She asked him if he'd heard anything from Lady Earth. "*Only that I'm king of the dragons. I don't know how I feel about that, but she's going to work with me in getting the training that I need about the laws, so I can rule. I guess there are a lot of them that even I'm breaking, but I get a pass on them because we didn't have any idea. Oh, and the faeries are staying, but not nearly so many of them. We can pare them down as much as we see fit to.*"

"*A quarter of them is still too many.*" She laughed with Kings. "*All right, I'll have to go over the book, too, I guess. This is really fucked up. When I think of all the things that had happened to you when you were younger, it makes me want to find your parents and beat them to death. I think I could do it too."*

"*I have no doubt that you could take them on and come out the winner. They've been terrible all my life, and I'm glad that they've been taken care of by the council. I don't know what happened to them, but whatever it was, it wasn't nearly enough.*" She agreed with him, and she hadn't been around when they were causing so much trouble. "*Trust me when I tell you that they would have tried to do something to you from the very beginning of our relationship.*"

After closing the connection she had with Kings, she decided that she needed a malt. Chocolate on chocolate ice cream. The others agreed, and even Kaida decided that she needed a brownie sundae. As they were seated eating their treat, she looked around the town and could see what other improvements needed to be done.

Someone had planted trees on the sidewalk. They had been pretty, she was sure, when they were first put in, but now that they were overgrown and too large, their roots breaking the concrete slabs, she could see the potential for someone getting hurt. The flags were still up from the Fourth of July. There were yards along the main street that needed to be cleaned up. Two of them had cars that had trees growing out of them. There were other things, too, some of them major, like the trees in the sidewalk, but there were little things, too. The library needed a new parking lot. There were empty buildings that needed to be boarded up because the windows had been broken out, and the glass was still there. This was all along Main Street, where she noticed this and not throughout the entire town.

"What are you thinking about that's going to cause me trouble?" She laughed with Ace, the more relaxed of the two brothers. "I was joking, but what were you thinking about?"

"This town has gone to pot." She pointed out the few things that she'd seen in the few minutes that she'd been looking and said she knew it was like that all over town. "Now that no more projects are going to be finished up, it's not difficult to tell what this town will look like in a few more years."

Ace looked around before speaking. "You can bet things like the streets will be the first to go. Then the schools. The schools will get funding from the state if it's needed, but if the town isn't viable, then there will be no one voting in the taxes that will be needed to maintain the buildings. Or pay for teachers. They're doing all right now, but like you said, in a few years, when there is just as much wear and tear going on with them, what they'll look like." He looked at her after taking one more glance around the streets. "Our town that we came from was just getting back on its feet. The sidewalks were being replaced. There was a new school going in. Also, the mayor there was working to keep the buildings that were falling down in good repair. You might be better off moving to where we live than staying here."

"You might be right." Her treat ruined now, she stood up and tossed it into the trash. "I'm going to go home and look for options on what to do when the town you grew up in is no longer a place you want to be." He told her he was sorry. "You didn't do it. It's the government that is around here. They've let things slack off for lack of a better term."

As she made her way home, she was feeling kinda depressed. So much was wrong with the town that she had to wonder if it was ever going to be a pretty little town again. It certainly didn't look like it from where she was standing.

~*~

Reading over the laws and rules that governed his kind, he couldn't believe how old some of them were. Like the second one he'd read said that they weren't to, under any circumstances, have anything to do with humans. There were several more like that, and he'd not even gotten to the third page yet.

There were instructions too on what to do with a dragon that needed to be beheaded. It was a long, drawn-out process that basically said stand back, cut their head off, and walk away. But there were fourteen steps that one had to follow before they could kill a dragon.

"Are you having any luck with that thing?" He turned to look at Tank, glad for the company. "I've seen that book before. I believe that every dragon was given a copy when they were just hatched. I don't remember reading it, but I remember someone giving it to me when I was little."

"Get this. You and your brother would have been killed when you were born—if you had been born, because you're not true dragons. Whatever the hell that means. And your mother wouldn't have been able to be a mate to your father either. Who would have been killed as a half breed. It mostly talks about what to do about humans and the rules we had to follow when we encountered them."

Kings snorted. "They outnumber us about fifty to one, and we're to avoid them in the event that we need to kill them later down the line."

"I think they outnumber us by a great deal more than that, my friend." Kings didn't comment as he was reading another little tidbit of information when a hatchling was changed into a dragon. Kings told him what the rule said. "It almost sounds as if we were never supposed to shift into humans at all, don't you think? I mean, how do we avoid them when we work with them or beside them daily?"

"I have no idea." Finally, Kings put the book down in order to talk to his new relative. "Skye said you were thinking of moving here. I have to say, after our conversation about the town, I don't know if I want to live here any longer. It's not like it can't be fixed, it can be, but it will take a great deal of money, I just don't see the town coming up with."

"If I were mayor, I'd start with the most dangerous ones first. Like the lift for the pool and the sidewalks." He asked about the pool and why to start there. "Because someone is going to think that swimming in a pool that has no lift for them is going to be a good idea and drown. That's all the city needs: a lawsuit that will be millions of dollars. Same with the sidewalk. I've seen them; they are a danger to anyone who wants to take a walk along them."

"What else would you do as mayor? I'm assuming that you've given this some thought." He told him what else he would do. "You know I was thinking the same thing. Why aren't the owners of these buildings boarding up their windows when they're obviously broken out?

Someone should have done that years ago. And not cardboard either. It needs to be really plywood covering them."

Kings started a list of things that they were talking about. Some of them were silly things, like the sidewalk needed to have yellow cones around the trees, and the school needed a bounce house on the premises so that they could keep track of the teachers who would be leaving when the funding dried up.

It was still being talked about when the others joined them for dinner. Cassian and Brenin laughed the hardest when they spoke about the mayor being taken out by tar and feathering him. However, it was Tucker who said that the mayor was running for reelection in the coming months, and it would be a perfect time for Ace to be put in the position.

"I was joking." No one wanted to hear how he'd been joking about becoming mayor and what he'd do. His ideas were spot on, and they were good ones to get them out of the situation they were currently in. "Look, I don't even know if we can live here or not, and I've got a full-time job as it is. What am I supposed to do if I have to run around policing the area every day until things look better here?"

"You'd get to live in the house for free, and from what I understand, it's a really nice house. I don't know if it's furnished or not, but it wouldn't be difficult to get that taken care of either. There's also a car that you have access to, as well as staff that the city taxes pay for. At least for now. But if you start the race by saying all the things that you're going to do without the funding from us, you'll be loved right from the start." He said that he didn't want to be loved; he had a job. "That you can literally do from anywhere and in about ten seconds. You said that it's no problem for you at all to find people and get things rolling in the direction that is needed. This would be the perfect job for you and your brother."

"How did I get involved in this?" Tucker pointed out that Ace was going to need an assistant. "But why me? I have a job too, remember?"

"You could both still keep your jobs now. I think that the only requirement to be mayor is that you attend so many meetings a month. And anyone that is having a luncheon or breakfast is the only time that the mayor— what the hell is his name anyway?" He was told. "His name is Morgan Trail? Did someone actually name him that?"

"Apparently, his parents had a good sense of humor." They all laughed about that as he was pulling the steaks and chicken off the grill. "I'm starving. All this talk about working has me worked up into starvation."

There was plenty to eat. The eight of them had choices of salads from green to potato and macaroni. Besides water and tea, there was wine that they could enjoy as well as juices. The cook had gone all out in making them things to go with the meal, and he couldn't have been happier.

After dinner, there were desserts as well. Ice cream, his favorite, as well as several different kinds of pies and two cakes, one chocolate and one yellow. Coffee was served along with more wine, and when they were finished with that, they went right back to talking about Ace becoming mayor for their little town. He certainly couldn't do any worse than the one they had in the position now, Kings thought.

When everyone was headed home, he had a feeling that they'd convinced Ace that the job would be perfect for him. It had a good pay with it as well as perks they didn't know of, too. As soon as he was up in the morning, he was going to take him downtown to fill out the application for running for the job. Hell, he'd even pay for all the signs that were going to be needed to keep him in office as well. It was going to be a good fit for everyone, and he thought that Ace wouldn't be in their pockets all the time, too.

There had been mention of funding that could be gotten for small towns to use. Once Cassian looked it up, there was even funding for the pool lift that could have been used to purchase and put in. Not to mention the empty buildings that were all along the main street that needed to be taken care of, and the sidewalks could be repaired as well. There were nonrefundable application fees that went along with it, but if you got the money, it would be so much more than what they were paying to apply.

All in all, it had been a fun night. He only hoped that Ace took them seriously about his running for the position of mayor. He'd be a perfect fit with them, and things would get done on a good timeline as well. That's just what they needed, too.

Chapter 6

The courtroom was packed, and there were hundreds of people still trying to get in from the outside. He'd not expected the crowds, as he didn't think that the Connors were well known around here, as they had been in another state altogether.

After the judge gave a lecture about how everyone was to conduct themselves during his trial, the couple was brought in. To say that they aged poorly would have been grossly overstated. They looked all of their years and then some. Even if you were to discount the fact that they were each wearing the drab orange of the jail system, they looked washed out, and she was heavier than he remembered her to be.

Jack Connor looked like someone's grandpa who had had a bad day. His hair was longer than his usual buzz cut, and it looked like he'd gone to bed with it wet and hadn't bothered to comb it out when he got up. The jumper that he had on looked stained, though it couldn't be told if it was fresh or not, but it was his hands that had startled Kings the most.

They were shaky and curled up in a claw-like look. His nails were long and dirty, like he'd been working in a garden and hadn't had time to wash up. He also had the smokers fingers were nicotine had stained his fingers because he'd been smoking for so long.

June didn't look much better, but instead of losing weight like her husband seemed to have done, she put on quite a few pounds. The outfit was ill-fitting and out of character for the older woman, as she seemed to be impeccably dressed the times that he'd seen her. Her hair was drawn back from her head tightly so that it looked, in certain lights, like she was bald. The silver of her hair was fighting vainly with the darkness of her roots, and it looked like the roots were winning.

They had put on the appearance of being a much younger couple so that no one would question the fact that they had a ten-year-old son, Trevor. They had changed his name from Trevor to Matthew Connors. And since he'd been no more than a baby at the time of the murder of his parents and kidnapping, he thought they were his parents for a long time. Then he'd run away and met up with Skye, who protected him as much as she could.

That's where Jason Waggoner had come into the picture. He'd been trying to find Skye to make her marry him. All he really wanted from her was her home and her paycheck, but she had left him, and the man had been chasing her since then. When Waggoner saw the young boy and remembered the pictures that he'd seen of him, he contacted the Connors, and they offered him a million dollars to bring the boy back to them, and he could do whatever he wanted with the girl. His plan then changed to killing her to get her out of the way so that he could get to the younger man.

But Kings discovered that she was his mate after helping her out of a situation at a diner where she was working, and she'd become someone that he would protect with his life. And that of Trevor, too. If he could, he'd adopt Trevor and make him his own son when he married Skye.

"Your honor, this travesty has gone on long enough. I've just spent the last five months in jail with my lovely wife. So whatever anyone thinks that we've done wrong, I think that we've more than paid for it." The honorable James Holden asked Jack if he thought that six months was long enough for a double murder. "I do, your honor. We should get some credit for not killing off the little boy, too. We raised him as our own. Our only sin is that we murdered his parents to have such a little boy. We love him."

"They would lock me into the basement and my room without food or water when I didn't perform for them correctly." The judge hit his gavel on the dais and asked for there to be quiet in his courtroom. "So you're all right with their lies? I'm not. They beat me, too."

"See here. We only beat you when you acted out. That's what any parent would do to their children. And we had reason for us to beat you and take away your privileges. You wouldn't do what we told you to do when there were others around." Jack looked at the judge. "He could tell what the stock market would be, and he wouldn't tell anyone that we had over what they would get if they invested in things. Plus, he kept telling people that he didn't belong to us. I don't know how he figured that out, but it surely made it embarrassing when he spouted off that stuff to near strangers."

"Both of you sit down in your seats. Believe it or not, I know how to run a courtroom and my word is rule. Now sit down and be quiet until someone speaks to you." Holden looked at Jack before continuing. "No, we don't beat our kids and take away their food and water when they act out. Nor do we lock them in the basement either. Now you keep your mouth closed until such time as someone asks you a question. Do you understand me?"

"Yes, but I don't like it." He told him how to address him. "All right, your honor, but as I said, I don't like this one bit. If this keeps up, not going our way, then I'm thinking that you're going to put us in some kind of bigger jail when we have already paid the price of killing off his parents. They weren't that good anyway. Always taking him away from me when I only wanted a few investments from him. What kind of person doesn't cash in on that when they have the golden egg right there in front of them? I'll tell you who. It was his parents, that's who."

"Are you finished? I'm asking you that so that I figure that once you talk yourself out, you'll finally do as I tell you and sit down and shut up." Jack said he was done for now. "The next time you have the feeling to take over my courtroom, I'm going to fine you five hundred dollars and ten days more in jail on top of jail time if there is any."

"Are you saying that we might not have any?" Holden told him that what he was saying was to shut up. "I will, but I don't have to like it. We've not been with our son Matthew now for too—"

"Who's Matthew?" The bailiff told the judge that was the name they'd given Trevor when they kidnapped him after murdering his parents. "His name is Trevor now, correct?"

"Yes, your honor." Finally, Jack sat down, but he wasn't quiet. He kept muttering under his breath about everything that was being said around him. Kings could hear him, and that made him think that if they ever got Trevor back, they'd kill him. Just from the few things that he had in his head, he knew it wouldn't bode well for the youngster if they were to get their hands on him again.

Witnesses were brought before the courtroom. Some of the people had some very damaging things to say about the Connor couple, and most weren't surprised by the fact that they'd killed Trevor's parents. Some were surprised that they were the only people that they had killed.

They were a black mark to their community and never did anything around their own property to make it look like the rest of the homes on their street. Going so far as to not mow their lawn all summer and leaving cars in the yard for things to live in it. There had been one family that complained of rats living on the land.

"Got nobody to mow it, now do I?" Jack was told to sit down again. "What does this have to do with us taking Matthew when we wanted him? Nothing I tell you. Not one thing. These people should be watching out. Something might befall them, too."

He was fined five hundred dollars and ten days added onto his sentence. Of course, that was something else he complained about. Not having a job nor anyone to help him with the investments meant that he couldn't pay anybody to mow his lawn and make the 'stupid people' of the town 'keep their traps shut' about his property.

At noon, the court recessed for lunch. The Connors

were taken back to jail; they'd worn out their welcome at the courthouse, and everyone else had an hour to come back. None of them moved as they knew that their seats were prime and they'd not have them when they returned. Sending out someone to get food for them was the next thing on their list. If they couldn't eat it in the courtroom, they'd go out two at a time to eat it before coming back for two more. They all wanted to be front and center in what was going on in the place today.

It was only a pre-hearing of the trial that might be months to years away. But they needed to know what was going to happen with Trevor. He was well-loved by the family, and all of them thought of him as a part of the family now. They only needed to make sure that they could adopt him before anyone tried to take him away.

"Jason is trying to wiggle his way out of his confession." He asked Brenin how he was doing that. *"He's saying that he was told to say that so he'd not have to go to prison. I don't know all the details, but a buddy of mine at the station house said that he's making all kinds of noise about Skye saying that she'd marry him, then backed out when things didn't go her way. Again, I don't know the details of that either, but I'm just letting you know what he's up to."*

"What do you suppose caused him to change his mind about the confession? He seemed proud of the fact that he'd been caught after killing so many people. Last I heard, he was going to write a book about how not to get caught. I think he said something along the lines that amateurs should never kill anyone to leave it up to the professionals." Kings asked how anyone was supposed to get to professional status when they didn't start with the first one. *"That's not a good*

question that I'd be going around asking if I were you."

"Yeah, I think you're right. It did make more sense in my head before I said it." He thought of something else but kept it to himself. The man had murdered thirty-five women, he'd told the police, and he'd never been caught. He'd even given the names and places where he got rid of the bodies. *"Keep me informed about Waggoner. We don't need any more surprises where he's concerned."*

For the rest of the afternoon, people were brought in who were friends of the couple who had been killed, the Warfield's. The young couple had been a nice addition to the town when they'd been alive. Outgoing and friendly. They'd even help out when they were needed with babysitting or snowplowing their driveways in the winter months. However, they never had anything good to say about the Connors. He would have hated to have been their neighbors. He might well have gotten into it with them as much as their neighbors did now.

As for Trevor, known as Matt back then, they couldn't believe that such a horrid couple had such a polite young man. And when he was out and about, he always looked so depressed. Now people understood why he had looked like that.

Waggoner was brought up, but not by name. It was June who had said they'd had to go to the expense of hiring someone to find their boy. The judge asked them how they were planning to pay the kidnapper, and they told them they were going to make Trevor tell them which stock to buy and sell so they'd be able to pay him. Jack said that a million dollars would have stimulated the economy a great deal if they'd been able to get the money. The judge just rolled his eyes.

In the end, there was enough evidence to have a trial for the couple. They were pissed off and made everyone at the stationhouse aware of their feelings about it, too, when they were told they'd have to go back to jail to await the trial, he'd heard from Brenin's friend. Tomorrow was going to be the pretrial hearing for Waggoner, and he was nervous about what he was going to say about Skye and the relationship she supposedly had with him.

But they'd be there tomorrow, or however long it took for him to be sent to jail, too. The Connors' date was mid-October, and hopefully Waggoner's would be around the same time. It would be good to get them over with at the same time, but he knew that was a long shot. With the number of witnesses that the prosecution had, it was going to be a long time in coming to hear if they were going to prison or not. Now all they had to do was wait for Waggoners' trial, and they'd be able to adopt Trevor.

Going home, they were headed to Brenin's home for dinner that night. He had wanted to try a new pizza place that had popped up seemingly overnight, and they were going to go there and share with him. Brenin was a food nut and would try things that he always thought should be left for someone else. He even liked kale.

Trevor asked to stay home, and they let him. He was only ten years old, but there was a houseful of staff there in the event something went wrong. He said that he wanted to finish a book he'd been reading, and Kings couldn't fault him there. Kings would rather read a book than just about anything in the world. Particularly when you were at the end of it.

~*~

"You know, I don't know that I would have ever thought of starting a fire with one of the dragons. That was brilliant of you." Skye thanked Kaida and told her that there wasn't any sense in wasting good flames. They both laughed. "It's nice that they can fly around without anyone taking shots at them. I know that it has to be at dark, but Tucker told me that they see better at night than they do during the day anyway. And it's good for them to be up there flying around. It makes them less stressed, I was told."

"Kings said that the other two cousins are non-dragons. I had to ask him what that meant. He said that while they had the superpower of dragons, they couldn't shift, and the other three had wind. I guess it's a powerful bit of wind, too. It could knock buildings over without much in the way of effort." The two of them were seated near a fire pit and enjoying the warmth coming off of it. Tucker had started it for them without shifting. It was one of his superpowers by having a mate. He had flames all the time. "Are you going to go to the courthouse in the morning?"

"I'm going. I've been called as a witness to testify against Jason." She told her that she'd not known that. "They called me the other day and asked if I'd be willing to do that. Trevor wanted to as well, but he's a minor, and they said they didn't want to traumatize him. I think what we went through was traumatizing enough."

"I've been meaning to ask you if you've heard anything more about the mayor position? Is Ace going to run against him?" She said that he'd filled out his application and filed it the other day. "We've been getting calls about him running. It seems people really want someone new in the position, and they don't seem to care who it is at this point."

"I heard that too. But Ace doesn't have any skeletons in his closet, so I'm not worried about that. But his being new to the area might be something that gets him fewer votes. Tucker is having fun with the campaign and getting posters made for him. I think he might never run for office, but he could certainly get your name out there when asked." She laughed and thought of how many signs she'd seen in other people's yards in the last few weeks. People really wanted someone else in the position. "I'm thinking that Mayor Trail might be in for a shocker with his posters saying that the best man is in office now. Ace will hopefully give him a run for his money."

They talked about the town and the list of things that Ace was going to fix when he was in office. She knew, too, that he was looking into grants and other things to bring in money so that the town could be brought back to its former glory. The sidewalks were the most important thing right now, as the pool had been closed up for a few weeks now, with fall coming on. She had a feeling that as soon as Ace was in office—if he won that is—that things would be fixed so quickly that it would be as if nothing was wrong. Ace had a good head on his shoulders.

"Did you hear that there is a company looking to purchase land not far from here? It's going to be in Zanesville, but closer to our end of town than downtown. I think that the factory makes sheets or something like that. Tucker has a friend who is also looking to expand his shirt and sweater company a bit more as well. They're here now, but they want tax breaks, too, or they'll just move to another town that will give it to them. That'll be a lot of jobs that will be lost because of it." She told Kaida that she didn't get around much, so she had missed that. "Tucker has his hands in a lot of things nowadays. Since the town was pointed out to him and how bad of shape it's in, he's been taking walks around the little town to see what else he can see that needs improvement. The school was able to get a grant that they're using for new computers for the teachers to use to teach classes. That was all on Ace. He took it to the school board meeting last week and got with the principal. He must have gotten on it right away because they heard back from them within a week."

"This town needs a newspaper. Or at least some kind of flyer that would tell good news like this. Don't you think?" She told her that they had a newspaper, but it only came out once a week, and by then all the good news was already spread around town by the people living here. "I've never seen it. I'll have to keep an eye out for it from now on. I wonder where I can find it."

She told her where she'd been able to find it. "I pick one up every time I go to the store. I don't know if there is a place in town you could get it, but then I've not been around as much as Tucker has been. I'll ask him. I'm betting that he has a good idea where we can get one."

Pulling out her phone, she made herself a list of things that she wanted to find. There were already several things on her list, but she wasn't worried about finding them. The next trip to Columbus would find her the special sheets she needed for their bed, and there were snacks that Trevor wanted that they just didn't carry around here. She loved that he was eating healthy and taking good lunches to the school he'd been going to.

"Did I tell you that Trevor is taking online college classes? He's struggling a bit, but I think because it's all new to him. He has to take a few classes of math that he couldn't test out of, but the pack school is helping him with the ones that he's taking. I think he even convinced the other nerds in his class to take some too." She asked about being called nerds. "They have formed a little group of Nerds of the Pack. I think it's great, and it's really helped his self-esteem too. I think that the Connors beat that out of him before, so I'm glad that he's getting it back. I've never seen a kid like him take to adults the way that he does now. He used to be so shy around them, but now he'll talk to anyone."

"So long as he's careful. I really love that kid. Did I tell you that he came over to the house the other day and helped my cook set up an online ordering application? We can all put something in the basket, then when she's ready to order, it all goes to the store, and they bring it to the house for us. They even bring it into the kitchen. The basket has been a big hit with Tucker as he's been looking for snacks himself that taste good and aren't too heavy. The guy burns about a million calories a day just walking, and he's worried about a few extra calories from some potato chips."

When the men started coming down from flying, she got a good look at their dragons. They weren't huge like she thought they might be, but not small either. About the size of a couple of school buses put side by side, not counting their wings. Their scales were shining, like they'd been polished by the moon's reflection off them. She thought that Kings were the most beautiful scales and his dragon was scary yet comforting too. She loved him so that might well have been it.

Once they were finished for the evening, they made sure that the fire was out so as not to cause any damage to any other place. Going into their homes, she was feeling kind of chilly because of the warmth outside and the coolness of the home. Getting a blanket off the back of the couch, she wrapped herself up in it to watch the late-night news before heading up to bed. Trevor came down just as they were locking up the house.

"I finished my book. I was wondering if I could go to the library tomorrow and see if I can get the second in the series." Kings told him that it would be great, and if they didn't find it at this one, they could search other libraries in the area to find it. "That's what he noted on the website said. I was told there are twelve other libraries that are attached to this one in town, and they had access to about a million books."

As she was getting ready for bed, her body seemed to be worn out. She told Kings what Kaida and she had talked about. He had questions about Waggoner and what he was up to, but she didn't have any more information than she'd given him. He said they'd have to wait until the morning to figure him out. Then she told him about the grant that the school had gotten.

"Now that I know about it, I've been helping Ace find all kinds of grants and other bits of money that can be used for all kinds of things. He said that the buildings on Main Street can be fixed up with a small business loan to the people who own the buildings. That'll be nice for them. However, they need to use the money for the buildings and nothing else, or they could go to prison for it. Kind of scary to know that borrowing money or even getting it for free could cost so much to your personal life if you fuck up." Skye agreed with him and then laughed. "What do you find so funny?"

"I was wondering what they'd do to the teachers if they fucked up with the money. Make them stay after class or write their name on the blackboard?" They both laughed then, and she sat on the side of the bed to wait for Kings. "I hope that Ace gets the job. Can you imagine the changes he'll make in his first few weeks in office? I know that he's been going around town and shaking hands with people. A lot of them like him even though he's not lived in this town for very long."

"It's fresh eyes and all that. He'll be able to see things that we've gone blind to and make them work for us. Also, I don't know if you heard, but the pool in town needs to have an upgrade. I'm not positive what that means for a hole full of water, but it needs to be done before the next season. He's looking into that as well." She said he's been busy. "You should see his little notebook. It's about full of things that people are telling him about that need to be fixed. I didn't even know that the town had a senior center, but they would like someone to come in and see to their furnace and air conditioner. I guess the air part has gone out in the summer, and they didn't have heat at the end of the winter last year."

Once they were in bed, they talked about his flying with his cousins. "I could see you flying around, but then

I knew you were up there. I wonder what someone would say if they were to see you guys flying around in the middle of the night. Would they be terrified or would they just say it's you guys and let it go?" He said they'd more than likely be afraid, as there were four of them flying around. "I can see that, too. I'd be terrified knowing something that big was just above my head, flying around. Do you ever lose a scale or something that would fall to the earth?"

"Mostly, they only come off during the spring. We'll lose a few, but they only come off on the ground. I've been using mine for different projects around the land around here. They make perfect shelters as they're waterproof and as hard as stone. If I were to build a building with them, it would be able to stand a tornado coming through." She said she wanted to see one the next time he had one to see. "I'll remember that for next time. They're very heavy, weighing in at about five hundred pounds for the larger ones and about a hundred for the smaller ones, up around my neck."

She was excited about seeing a real scale, but turned on her back to look up at Kings when he said her name. "I've been thinking a great deal about our child. I'm going to see if I can contact some older dragons to see what it's going to be like for you. I mean, I know that you have an egg, and it grows with the dragon that's inside of it. But that's all I know. I don't know even how long you would carry one, much less anything about it being born to us."

"I'd love that information. I've been thinking about how we're to keep him or her around if they're born a dragon. Or because I'm part human, will they be born as a child? I have no idea what to expect, and that's sort of scary." He said that he'll put the word out tomorrow for some answers to what they both need to know. "Do you suppose there are a lot of dragons still around? I mean, other than you six?"

"I don't know. I know that there are some of ours that are second-generation cousins. But as far as where they might be, I don't know. I've asked the others, including Ace and Tank, and they don't know either. None of us has our parents around anymore, thanks to them fucking up, but that's all right with us. We didn't care much for them in the first place. Especially Tucker's parents. They're dead now, but they were the worst of the worst kind of people. They ignored him until he was twenty-five years old, then sent him on his way. He had a sister, too, who was just as bad to all of us."

After snuggling down under the covers, the two of them stopped talking and began the process of going to sleep. She had to check off her list of things that she was able to get done today, and that made her relax enough that she could fall asleep. And she was out. It didn't take long for her to be asleep after the days that she'd been having around the town.

Chapter 7

Jason decided that he wasn't going back to jail. And in order for that to happen, he was going to have to commit suicide by cop. But he thought getting this lot of officers to do anything like that was about a million to one, not in his favor. They didn't seem to get riled up by anything that was going on around them.

Like the other day, one of the Connors had decided that their meal wasn't what they wanted. Instead of asking for something different, she threw their plate at the officer, and it hit him square in the face. All the cop did was wipe his face off with his hand and walk away. Nothing. No shouting. No cursing. Nothing to indicate at all that he was pissed off about what had just happened. And instead of June being without her meal, he simply brought her another plate of food and left. Crazy shit like that was going to get someone hurt.

Today, he was going to his pre-trial at the courthouse. He'd been warned several times that it was going to be today, but he just didn't want to believe it. There had been more important things that he wanted to take care of, and this wasn't it. He wanted out of this jail before the courthouse, and now it looked like it wasn't going to happen.

"Wagoner, you have fifteen minutes before we leave. Whatever you have left lying about will be boxed up for you if you are sent on to prison to await trial." He said he didn't want his fucking things touched. "They'll be put in a box for you to take with you, and that's final. If you have anything that doesn't belong to you, we'll find it then and return it to the proper owner."

See? He asked himself. He'd just said he didn't want his things touched, and they acted like he'd not said a word. Like they were above getting upset when someone cursed at them. Stupid people. He just wanted to blow all their heads off.

When he was told to step back in the cell against the wall, he did so without hesitation. He'd seen what happened to you when you didn't listen to that bit of advice. They brought in the hose and hosed you down with it until you complied. It was cold out, and he didn't want to be freezing his nuts off while on his way to the courthouse anyway.

Once he was cuffed up and ready to go, he walked by the Connors' cells. They were across from each other and would talk all hours of the night about how they were going to get that boy back and have him help them make some real money. He no longer believed that they had a million bucks; had they had it then, they'd be out on bail and not sitting in this shitty hole waiting on the judge to come and talk to them. He'd also heard that their trial was going to be sometime in the fall, and he wasn't going to be hanging around that long either.

The jail wasn't shitty by any means. It was cleaned once a day by someone who came in to do it. The man would take out the trash and run a mop over the floors. He would then leave you clean linens when he removed the ones from your bed. He didn't get that kind of service when he was staying at a five-star hotel when out on the road.

Even the food was good here. There were eggs and bacon for breakfast. Some kind of sub or sandwich for lunch, sometimes even a bowl of soup that wasn't watered down. For dinner, you had to pick if you wanted chicken or beef, and they'd bring you mashed potatoes with your meal and warm rolls. He thought they were getting it from the diner in town, but wasn't sure. It had only been the three of them in the cells since he'd been arrested.

It was all Skye's fault that he'd been caught. If she would have just died like he had tried to get her to do, then he'd have the boy, and that would have been the end of it. In hindsight, he didn't think he would have given the boy over to the Connors. They were too hyped up to have him making them some money for him to believe that they'd give him the million dollars they promised him for his work in getting him. Then Skye had messed that up, too. She was like a cat with fifty lives, the way she kept getting one step ahead of him every time he thought that he'd killed her ass.

One time, he noticed that she was driving a car. Where it had come from, he never knew, but there were people always helping her out of one jam after another. Cutting the lines to the breaks had done the trick, he thought, but when he'd seen her driving it for the next week, he knew that someone was watching out for her. There was no way that she'd been able to know that the lines had been cut and that she was going to die in a horrific accident. It was things like that that would piss him off to no end.

And the boy, too. He would swear that he had the kid in his hands several times, only to find him not being there. He had trapped the boy in a house, all exits were locked, and he would search the house, and he'd not be there. Not only wouldn't he be there, but it looked as if he'd taken all the things with him that made it so he could live there. No clothing, no shoes. Nothing to say that anyone had been living in the house. Damn it all to hell and back, it wasn't fair the way they kept getting away from him like he wasn't the best that there was.

The ride over to the courthouse wasn't long, but it did give him a different view than his cell had given him. He had a window with bars on it that didn't budge, but all he could see was the parking lot where the employees parked their cars at the station house. He could see where houses had been decorated with fall pumpkins as well as scarecrows in their yards. Jason didn't have any idea when Halloween was, but he figured that it was coming up on time for the kids to be out getting candy and such. Remembering it from his childhood, he smiled a little. It had been the only time all year that he'd get something for nothing, and he hoarded that candy like it was the crown jewels and there was a thief out on the loose.

He wouldn't have a costume or anything along those lines. But he had his pillowcase ready to receive the goods when he went from house to house. Jason had been good about it, too. Telling folks thanks and have a nice night, even when they only gave you one piece of bubble gum. That had been the time when he was happiest. Out of the house he'd grown up in and out among people who were just trying to get by like he was. But his parents fucked that all up for him when, one day, coming home from school, the police were there.

His daddy had killed his momma and then himself. The police told him that he'd been lucky he'd been at school that day, or he might have been a victim too. He did think of himself as lucky right up until he was put in the system as unadoptable. He'd been too big for his age and looked like a man at thirteen. Going from house to house had him wishing that he'd been home that day and had been a victim like the officer had told him he'd been.

"We're here. Don't give the judge any shit, or he'll send you right back to jail. He's not in the best of humor after yesterday with the Connors, and it won't take much to get him going again today." He didn't say anything, thinking that it was good that the man was in a sour mood. It would suit him just fine in his own plan of getting himself dead today. Going back to prison wasn't going to be an option for him anytime too soon. "Keep your mouth shut unless spoken to."

Safe advice, he thought, but Jason was out of safe options. He thought of all the things he was going to say today to get himself in trouble and sent back to jail in a body bag. Or something along those lines.

The courthouse was packed full of people, even standing around the outside edges. He wondered what was going on when he caught a glimpse of a couple of people he thought he knew. Damned if it wasn't Skye done up in some fancy-ass clothing and that boy that he'd been trying to get. Christ, it was something to see when a few bucks' worth of clothing would make you shine like the two of them were doing.

The men around them were big suckers, and he could only assume they were the Savage family. He couldn't see their faces very well; he'd been plagued with farsightedness for a long time, and they were simply too far away. But he did get a good look at the one that seemed to be handling Skye.

He was treating her like she was something precious, and there wasn't going to be anyone getting to what he considered his. Jason wondered if anyone would look at him like the man looked at Skye. Christ, it was damned near sickening, he told himself with a bit of jealousy.

When the courtroom was called to order, he continued to stand after everyone else was seated. He had some things he needed to say, and he wasn't going to wait his turn to do it. Jason had been practicing his speech since he'd gotten arrested. He wanted out, and this was the only way to do it. He was asked what he wanted to say.

"I'm not going back to prison. You can tell me that I'm going, and I'll do everything within my power to make it not happen. Even if I have to go after you, too." The judge asked him what he thought was going to happen when he'd confessed to killing thirty-five women and ten men. "I don't care what happens about them. I'm not going back. You might as well kill me now as to send me back there because I'm going to do my damndest to get in a body bag if that's what your plan is."

"Well, son. I appreciate your candor, but I don't sentence people at pre-trial. This here is a hearing to see if they have enough evidence to have yourself a real trial. I have to say, with you confessing, it sure is going to put a damper on your day in court." He said that he was made to say that about his confession. "Don't matter a hill of beans to me either. I'm sure now that you've given the courts enough to hang you with, they'll be able to put you behind bars for a while now."

"They coerced me into confessing. I didn't do any of those things." The other attorney stood up and said that the police were looking into the deaths that Mr. Wagoner was talking about, and since he'd been able to give them the places that he'd buried the people at, they were digging them up as we speak. "They're just lucky, that's all. I didn't do it."

"That's what I'm here to figure out. If they got themselves enough to have a trial over." The man wasn't listening to him, and that was starting to piss him off. "Now you have a seat right there, and we'll get this started and maybe have you back to your cell before too much longer."

"I'm not going to prison." He said that they'd see about that and laughed a little. "Do you think that I'm funny in some way? I'm telling you that I'm going to do whatever it takes to keep myself from going to prison. I'm not going back."

He looked around the room then and noticed that about half the people had left. He didn't know where they were going, but it seemed to him, too, that he had a wide circle of freedom around him. Looking when the doors opened in the back, the room began to fill with the officers who had just brought him in. It looked like the judge was taking him more seriously than he'd thought he was.

"Nobody in here wants to get hurt today. Why don't

you have a seat, and these nice officers will take you back to your cell. That way, you can be told later today how things are going for you. But as I've said to you already, I'm not going to sentence you today, as this is just a pre-trial. You know, to see if they have enough evidence to try you at a later date. Now, what I can do is to make sure you're not taken to prison right away if you cooperate. You let them come to you and they'll hustle you out of here right quick and back to the jail where you'd been spending your time." He said that he'd been coerced into saying what he did. "Then they'll not find any evidence to take you to prison on. We just have to take care of the issue of you trying to kidnap Mrs. Savage right here and that boy, Trevor."

They were going to find the bodies as he had confessed like a fool to killing those fifty or less people. He'd been bragging and thinking that they'd be as lazy as any other jail he'd been in, that they'd not check on it. For him, thinking that these people never got their dander up, he was certainly wrong about these people. They weren't lazy, they were slick, and he didn't like being wrong about people.

When he felt someone behind him, he nearly lunged, but he was stopped by the sheer size of the man. He looked like he weight lifted houses, he was so fucking big. He wasn't armed either, but standing there in his shirt sleeves and dress pants like he'd just come from some kind of business meeting.

"You're not going to give me any trouble." He nodded before he could get his head to understand that this man would and could kill him if he just snapped his fingers. "No, you're not. I'm going to put you in a lock hold and you're going to cooperate with the officers."

Before he could figure out what a lock hold was, the big man had his arms around his neck and his hands shoved up behind him. He couldn't breathe, much less move, when he was held like this. As soon as the officers got close enough to touch him, Jason kicked out, using up all the air he had in his body and passing out.

When he woke up, he was not just in his cell, but he was chained to the bed as well. All his things were boxed up outside the cell. Not that he could get to them, not how he was chained up, but he knew that as soon as he could, he was going to sue the department for abuse. That was the only thing that he could think of to say why he'd ended up in his cell again.

As he moved around, there was enough chain for him to stand up, but not much more. He felt the only thing that hurt was his head. And it was pounding like someone had used him for a punching bag at some point. It wasn't a sickening one, but it hurt badly enough that he thought he might be if he had to move around too quickly. Christ, who had that man been?

~*~

"What if you had gotten hurt?" Tucker told Skye that he was an immortal, that he might have broken a nail, but nothing more would have happened to him. "I don't care about your stupid nail. I'm talking about being hurt really badly. Immortality doesn't keep you from getting hurt, you know."

"I didn't want the officers to get hurt, so I was a distraction for him. I never thought that I'd have to wrangle him, too. But he went down pretty easily, and no one was hurt. Not even me." She said she was still upset with him. "If it helps you at all, I talked to Kaida about it, and she was fine with me helping them out. She did care, however, if I broke a nail while helping them."

"Because she's in love with you." He asked her if she loved him, too. "I do, but like I said, it doesn't negate the fact that you could have been hurt."

"I promise you the next time the police need my help, I'll ask you first." She smacked him on the arm. "That hurt. See? You hurt me more than I was hurt helping the police. He really wasn't any trouble. I was surprised that he went down so easily. After hearing him talk about how badass he is, I expected more of a fight from him. But all he did was kick out, and that was it."

"Ms. Savage, he might well have gotten one of our guns in that mess. It's happened before, I've heard. You think that someone is going to be a pussycat, and you find out that they're meaner than a rattlesnake. And slick too. He would have done us some serious damage had he gotten a hold of one of our guns. Or even if he was to have gotten one of us in a choke hold like Mr. Tucker was talking about, then we'd have had to pull our guns out and shoot him. That would have been messy, and a dead man would have been on the courthouse floor. Can you imagine the mess all that blood and bullets would have done to the floor in there?" She could only stare at him as that was the most anyone of them had said in all the time she'd been around them. "All I'm saying is that without his help, it would have been a mess of a mess. We'd be mopping up blood from now until the building needed to be replaced."

Tucker was all right, and that was what she should have been focusing on, but she could still see the evil in Jason's eyes when he was being held by Tucker. Shivering, she knew that she'd have to keep an eye on Kings to make sure he didn't try to one-up his cousin. He'd do something equally terrifying for her, and she'd have to smack him around a bit, too.

They had stayed for the rest of the hearing. Or pre-trial, whatever they wanted to call it. Jason was going to prison. Of the forty or so places that he'd given them where people were buried, the police had already dug up half of them. And they were precisely where he said they'd be, too.

Some of the bodies had been shot, and some had had their throat slit, according to the medical examiner who had started on the bodies. There were a few that had been strangled, too. She didn't know how they could tell that on a body that had been in the ground for as long as some of them had been, but she wasn't going to quibble. He had confessed to killing them, and that's all she cared about.

"Did you ever think about what he might have done to you had you been killed by him?" She asked the officer why he'd say something like that to her. "Just wondering. He's a nasty man and a killer. I, for one, am glad that he's been caught before he could do any more harm to anyone. I wonder what drove a man like that to kill. From all accounts, he's been doing it since he was in his twenties. What is he now? Forty-five? Fifty?" He looked at her. "Makes you wonder what's going through his head all the time. Don't it?"

She walked away from the officer. He was too much for her. As soon as she got outside in the cooler weather, she put her face up to the sun and let it warm her suddenly cold skin. He might well have killed her, and that right now was all she could think about.

"Skye?" She turned and smiled at Kings. "We were going to grab some dinner and head home if you want. I know that movie you wanted to watch on television has finally dropped to be streamed."

"I just want to spend time with you and Trevor." He said that Trevor was spending the night with the troop tonight. "I forgot about that. I wish he could get out of it. Seeing Jason today has made me realize how lucky we were to have run into you, and you saved us."

"You're still worried about Tucker, aren't you? You know that they had his back? Nothing would have happened to him even if Jason had gotten away. He'd be dead, which is what I think he wanted to happen, but Tucker never would have been harmed. He would have stepped back had he not been able to hold him, and that would have been the end of his involvement in the whole thing." She said that Jason wasn't a normal prisoner nor a normal man. "No. He's not. But like I said, the police had his back and nothing would have happened to him."

"Let's go home." She waited in the car while he went in to get their dinner. They were going to have to start eating at home more, or they'd be as big as houses soon. Then she remembered what Kaida had told her about not being able to gain any weight unless they were breeding. She put her hand over her still flat belly and smiled. "I wish I could count the days until you get here, love. I don't even know if I can get prenatal care with you being part dragon."

When Kings came back, he told her about the woman he'd been talking to about birthing baby dragons. She was coming to visit next week to see how she was doing and to give her any information that she could. She wasn't a dragon either, but had birthed five of them when her husband had been alive. The only reason that she'd not been immortal like most dragons was because she'd not figured that her husband loved her enough for all eternity, and regretted that ever since.

"When she didn't want to be immortal, he had someone take his immortality away so that they could live out their life as a couple. Then, about five years after that, he was killed in a car accident that took the lives of three other people. She said that she regretted it since then that she didn't have him around forever." She told him that it was a sad story. "It is, isn't it? When I heard her story, I wanted to hug her tightly and tell her that it would be all right."

"I'm going to do that very thing when we see her." The drive home was made in record time, and once they were there, she had Kings light the fireplace, and they ate their dinner right there in the middle of the floor, close to the flames. She seemed to be cold forever, while just Kings feet would get cold. He said he felt it through his entire body when that happened. "Tell me what will happen to Jason now."

"You mean other than he'll go to prison? He'll be put on a watch so he doesn't kill himself. He's confessed to not wanting to go to prison again, and this will be his third time. I don't know which one he'll go to be incarcerated in, but that's where he's going to be headed." Skye asked how long did he think he was going to get. "I'd say at least a few life sentences. Whether or not he'll get parole or not is going to be the big question. He took more than one life, so it's hard to say what will happen with that."

"But you're sure he's going to get prison." He pointed out that he'd threatened a sitting judge, too, and that wasn't going to go over all that well. "I'd forgotten about that. He did say he was going to get him if that's what it took for him to get out of going to prison. To be honest, when he said that, I wasn't sure what he was talking about. If he were to have done that, they would have killed him. I guess that's one way to get out of going to prison. Do you really think he would have done that?"

"I do. It would be his third time going back. I don't know what that means, but he's had to have had a good view of what prison life is like because of that." She nodded, feeling like they should change the subject. "How about we get some of our work done for this week and get to bed early for tomorrow? It's supposed to rain all day with spits of snow perhaps by midnight."

It took her a while to get caught up on the things that she'd put off for the last two days. Working from home, she was still missing a lot of the house in what needed to be done. The other bedrooms were finished up now, and Trevor had a lovely desk that he'd been wanting. Getting her work done took a bit longer because she kept stopping to think about what Tucker had done for the police.

While she knew that he was an immortal, she

had still worried about him being involved. What if the next time the police needed his help, and it was a more dangerous person they were dealing with? Or the person actually was armed? A gun could do a lot of damage when someone was desperate. She knew why he'd done it, it was really to save the officers from being hurt, but the next time, he might not be so lucky. While thinking of Tucker, she went to find Kings to tell him that she loved him.

His head was bent over his desk, and he looked to be working really hard. It wasn't until Ace spoke that she knew he was on the phone with someone. They were going over the list of things that needed to be seen to when he became mayor. The special elections were in about ten days, and it looked like he was going to win. If Trails' desperate attempts to get out there with the people were any indication, he knew that Ace was going to win as well.

Instead of bothering him about her insecurities, she went to her office again. Doing the books for the dragons wasn't all that difficult, but she wanted to make sure that she was on top of it all the time. They spent a great deal of money every day, keeping up with charities and the like, so she made sure that there was still money in the bank if they wanted to pay for a candy bar. It would never get that bad, but it was something that she wanted to keep on top of every day.

Letting time get away from her again, she was headed up to bed around midnight. But she'd gotten a great deal of work done, more than she'd thought that she would have when she first sat down, and was looking forward to sleeping in tomorrow. While she rarely slept past eight o'clock, she thought that sleeping in until ten would be heaven. Smiling as she brushed her teeth, she was sliding into her bed at just after twelve-thirty when Kings joined her.

"Ace is getting nervous about the election. He said that he doesn't know if he can do it." She snorted, and Kings laughed. "Yeah, that's what I told him, too. I also mentioned that he had this in the bag, but he wouldn't believe me. One minute he's talking like he won't win, then the next breath he's afraid that he will win. There is no pleasing some people, is there?"

"I noticed that someone has marked the worst area of the sidewalks. Did he do that, or did the police finally get involved?" He said that he'd not noticed. "It's big red paint. Might be for the trick-or-treaters to avoid the place."

"I'm betting that's it. I wouldn't want anyone to be hurt around those, and like you said, if they mark them up, then maybe someone will take notice and be more careful." She said that Kaida had ordered flashlights that she was giving away with her candy. Then, they asked if they had any treaters that might come to their home. "I don't know. I guess we should get some just in case. I've not lived here all that long, so I have no way of judging. I don't believe I've ever given out candy before. Have you?"

"When I was younger. I don't know if Trevor has ever been on the receiving end of treaters, either. I wonder if he'll think he's too old for it this year. I think he's at the perfect age." He agreed as he got into bed. "Any more news about you being king of all dragons?"

"Nothing so far. I have a meeting again with Lady Earth. She's supposed to give me a book or two that were with the previous king. I did wonder what happened to the faeries that were supposed to have been training me, but we've been so busy that I've not had any time." Skye asked if he would ask her. "I thought about it. And I don't think I want to know. So long as everyone knows that none of this is my fault, then I'm all right with not knowing."

Snuggling up with Kings, she knew that tomorrow would bring more questions about Jason and the Connors. Right now, she was happy for the answers that she had now and was glad that someone was taking an interest in their cases enough to keep them off the streets.

Chapter 8

It didn't take long for the courts to come back with Waggoner, and the Connors were going to go to court. It was iffy if they were going to be spending their time in the local jail or a prison. Kings thought that they should all three be put in prison and never thought of again. But he wasn't in charge of the jail system, just dragons.

Lady Earth had given him more books on what his new role as king of dragons was going to be like. There were a great many laws that needed to be deleted or updated in most of the books he'd been given. The one that he thought needed to be gotten rid of was that dragons could only marry within their kind. He wondered just how many dragons had broken that law besides himself and Tucker.

There were laws about dues to be paid. One percent of their yearly income didn't seem like a great deal, and it wasn't. However, where was the money going? As far as he could tell, it was sitting in some vault somewhere gathering dust instead of interest. That was on his list of things to look into when he finished going over the books.

There were a total of five books that were his to use. Two of them were how he was to conduct himself when there was an outing or an event. The outing could have been him just walking into town, but there were rules that he was supposed to be using, and he couldn't seem to wrap his head around them.

There was a crown that he was to wear at all times when he was in his human form. It had been made of the finest jewels and sat upon a crown made of gold. He'd not seen it as yet and hoped, like a lot of things that he was reading, that it wasn't found because there wasn't any way that he was going to start wearing a crown at this stage of his life. Not to mention the 'finery' that he was to wear to go with it. He was still going through the second book when Skye joined him in his office.

"Do you know what a pip is?" He told her it was a group of faeries. "Why are they sometimes called a horde? I mean, I understand both words now, but I don't know what the difference is."

"I'm not sure either. But we're to have a pip in our house at all times. Something about making our lives better." She snorted. "Yeah, I'm right there with you on that. They've done nothing but disturb our lives since the first time they arrived."

"Did you know that they have special magic that comes because they work in our home? It's to protect us from unwanted enemies. I can't understand why we'd want enemies. Aren't all enemies unwanted? I mean, doesn't it sound like that to be true?" They both laughed, and she came and sat down on the corner of the desk he was behind. "I've been reading over the first book you gave me. How are we going to have any dragons left if we enforce even half the rules in that sucker? We'll have to either jail them all or kill them because of most of the rules in that book."

"I've been going over some of them with Lady

Earth, who I like by the way. Oh, before I forget, the pip that was supposed to be training me has been punished. Not killed but punished for lying to the Lady all this time. Apparently, they were supposed to have trained me on these rules that we're just now getting, and I was to be working as the king apparent." Skye asked him how they were punished. "I don't know. She told me that it was appropriate for the crime. Whatever that means."

"I'm going to let it go. There's nothing I can do about it, so I'm not going to try. She has handled it, and that's the end of it for me. How about you?" He said he was thinking the same thing. "Good. At least we can agree on that one thing. But these rules kind of make me nervous. I'm not a dragon, and we're mates. Punishment for that rule is that we both be put to death. How do you even kill a dragon?"

"Removing their head. Mostly it's done when they're human, but it can be done as a dragon too. Just a bit harder, I guess." She nodded and stood up. "Do you have any plans for the day? I'm going to be stuck with this for the rest of my life, I think."

"We have a formal dinner at the Lady Earth's castle. I've never been to a castle before, have you?" He told her that he grew up in one. "How nice. But I don't imagine that the one you grew up in had all the niceties as the ones that are in my head, did you?"

"We didn't have running water or bathrooms like we have today. If that helps you think of how we grew up." She shivered, and that made him laugh. "It wasn't all bad. The kitchen help would wash things in the same water that they cooked with. How's that image?"

"Enough. I hope that her castle at least has clean water. I don't want to be sick the first time I enter one." She went to the window and looked out over the yard. He knew what she was seeing, and it did his heart good to know that they got themselves a good home with a wonderful backyard. He asked her what was wrong. "I hope you're not being bogged down with all this reading. If so, you should call Kaida and have a lunch meeting with her. I'm sure that she'd love to get out of the house, too."

"She's busy with Tucker. They're going over the charities that they donate to. When I was helping with their books, I noticed that a lot of the charities they donate to are no longer in business. I marked a few of them, but there are more that I don't know anything about. I did wonder where the money was going."

"That happens to us since we've been around for so long. We invest in things and, over time, forget about them. Mostly it's not a great deal of money that we've been paying into a fund, but after a while it does add up." She said that's what she found when going over their books for them. "Maybe we should have you go over ours. There is no telling what you might find out about what I've been paying into after all this time."

"I'll gladly do that." She still looked pensive, and he closed the book he was working on and told her to come to him. "If I do, then I'm going to start crying, and I'm too emotional to stop if I get started."

"I can handle it. Come here, baby, and allow me to hold you." She was crying before she got to him. And he'd lied to her; there was no way that he could handle the tears that she was shedding. "I love you, honey. Tell me what's wrong so that I can slay the knight in shining armor."

"You're supposed to slay the...oh. I guess you'd have to slay yourself if that were true. I don't know what's wrong with me. Maybe it's the baby. Have you gotten any information from that woman yet?" He reached for a book and handed it to her. "You had this all this time and didn't think to give it to me?"

"I just found it this morning. It was bundled up with the rest of the books that were dropped off." She opened the book and read a few lines to him. "Well, that tells you something. You'll carry the child for six months, then a year before it's a hatchling. We didn't know that."

"It says here that no matter which one of us is the dragon, the child will be born a dragon. We know that's not true. Look at Ace and Tank. They're both human-like from their parents." He explained how they were only born of a half-dragon and a human. "So the further down the scale is from one of them being a dragon, the harder it is to tell what will be born. I suppose you're all dragon down through the ages."

"I am. But you have to remember that I was born a very long time ago, when that was the norm for dragons to marry and mate with dragons. I think that statement about the baby being born a dragon with you is going to be true, however." She left him at his desk and sat in one of the chairs that were across from him. "All better now that you have some information?"

"I am, thank you very much." He watched her as she read through another couple of pages. "It says that I have to eat more red meat. And to drink more juice. I already do that. I also have to take naps when I need to because it's draining carrying a dragon baby. I think it would be draining carrying any child, don't you?"

"I do." He watched her a bit more and smiled when her brow seemed to be making creases. "What have you found now? Something that I can help you with? Or is it something that you have to do on your own?"

"It says I need to have a nesting place for the egg or eggs. I never thought about me having more than one baby before. Can you tell?" He said that he couldn't, but maybe Lady Earth could tell. "I'll have to ask her what she thinks. What's a nesting place?"

"I honestly have no idea." She just stared at him. "You have to remember that I'm an ancient and haven't been around babies in longer than I can remember my childhood." She told him she didn't know babies either. "Well, together we'll figure this out. We'll just have to go with the flow of things and figure them out as we go. What do you think?"

"I think we might be in over our heads here." He laughed, and she glared at him. "When this baby is born, you're going to be helping me as much as I do. This will be our project that we learn from if you want to have any more than just the one."

"I'll be helpful. From what I've read, too, the faeries will be helpful as well. That is one of the reasons that they'll be around is for any children that we have." She asked what they could do; they were so tiny. "But there are a lot of them. And don't forget they have magic as well. And when the babies start coming, they'll have even more, so that they can protect him when we need them to. Sort of like a nanny with guns kind of thing."

"I like that. Nannies with guns. I can almost see them standing guard over the crib with their guns out and their little wings flapping. I think someone coming to hurt the baby wouldn't be able to stop laughing long enough to do any harm, and we'd be able to subdue them. What do you think?" He said that it would be a sight to see. "Do you think we'll be good parents? I don't have a great deal of role models on my side, and you don't have it either. How about we just raise them in the opposite way that we were raised and hope for the best?"

"Is this what has you so sad? You don't think you're going to be a good parent?" She nodded, and her lower lip quivered some. "Oh, Skye, you're going to be the best. Even if you don't have the book with you, you'd do fine. I know it. Any baby would be lucky to have you as a mom. Just look at how good you've done with Trevor. I know he wasn't a baby when you and he hooked up, but you've done a great job in keeping him safe and fed." He turned in his chair to pat his lap. "Come here and let me hold you."

She came across the room and sat on his lap. Holding her always made him feel better, too, and when she wrapped her arms around him, he felt like he could take on about anything and come out the winner. After a few minutes, he realized that she was asleep and continued to hold her in his arms while she rested. She hadn't been sleeping well, and he knew that it had a lot to do with all the sex they were having. He was going to have to slow down or she'd be worn out to a nub before their first anniversary. Smiling to himself, he was ready to doze off when a faerie came into the room.

"Your lordship, may I have a word with you? It's about the household staff." He whispered that they had no household staff. "The other faeries. I do believe that there are too many of us for a house this size. We expected you to be living in a much larger space."

"I had a much larger space, but I downsized to this one because I didn't need all that extra. This house suits us both very well. I know that when the children come along, we'll have to go bigger, but for now we'll be living here." He nodded and said that he understood. "What's wrong with sending some of the pip back?"

"They wish only to serve, my lord. So I was wondering if you had an idea what to do with so many of us staying here with you." He started to tell them that he had enough on his mind right now to deal with something else, but then he thought of something else. "They have been chosen to come to you and have been so proud of the fact that they can serve their king of dragons and his mistress."

"Send them to my cousins so that I can be assured that they're safe as well. It would be a great honor for me for some of them to go to their homes and make sure they have the same care that we have here." The little wings on the faerie started fluttering faster. Hopefully, that was a good sign. "Tell them that it's my wish to share this good omen with them so that they'll be as happy as I am with my faeries."

"That is most excellent, my lord. Yes, I'll divide them up so that they'll each have the perfect amount of them in each of their homes." Nodding, he was trying his best not to be giddy with the excitement of having one less thing that he had to worry about. "I will do that posthaste. If you will tell the others what a great gift you have given them, then we shall spread out today if possible."

"I'll take care of that now." He hoped they would take it as it was meant, a gift to them so they'd have the same magic around as he did. Because the faeries really did have their own kind of magic, and it spilled over into their lives, too. "You just make sure that they all understand that this is something that I wanted so as to make my cousins feel as good as I do about having you guys around."

"I will, my lord. I'll make sure that they are aware of what a great gift you are sharing with them." When he fluttered away, mumbling to himself, Kings adjusted Skye in his arms to hold her better. Before he got too comfy and fell asleep with her, he reached out to his cousins to tell them the good news. Or he hoped they'd think of it as good news.

~*~

"What the hell am I supposed to do with a bunch of faeries?" Cassian didn't like that Kings was laughing. *"I just got my house situated, and now you're going to share this great bounty that I've heard nothing but complaints from you about them, too. Why are you really doing this?"*

"Seriously, I didn't want to hurt their feelings. And you guys could use a little help now and then with your houses. Did I mention that they clean up after you, no matter how messy you've been in the kitchen? That's a plus right there if you ask me."

"No one asked you anything. You're doing this to become

more friendly with the faeries while making enemies with us. I see how you are. You're just trying to make our lives more difficult." Kings told him if he didn't want them there, then tell them when they arrive. "Oh yeah, make me the bad guy in this. What if I told you that you're not to send them? What would you do then?"

"They're coming. Probably on their way right now." Cassian listened as his brother Brenin complained about having the extra help around the house. "It'll be just fine, you'll see. And I didn't complain about them that much. It's just that there are so many of them. You've been here. Just think. You'll only have about one-sixth of what I had in my house. That should count for something for you."

The others weren't complaining as much as he thought they might, and he figured that since it seemed like it was a done deal, then he should just deal with it. It would be nice to have a few extra hands around the place when he was vegging in front of the television at night and left himself a mess for in the morning. Also, he hated to dust. Maybe they'd take that over, too. Not to mention the windows being washed when they needed it. He was starting to warm up to the idea, but wasn't going to tell Kings. Instead, he was going to let him think that he was doing him a favor by taking on the faeries. It might get him a bonus later down the line, like a favor that he could ask for and get from the big dragon.

"I'll take them, but you're going to owe me." Kings said that he was all right with that, too. "Good. I want you to remember that, too. That we did you a favor in taking on – how do you pay them? I mean, they get paid for being around us, don't they?"

"*We gave them a place to put their homes in the house. Not all of them, because that would be just too much, but the few that are staying. Also, you need to put out fresh flowers when you can get them; they eat the blooms. And sugar cubes too. Not too many of those, or they'll get sick. They don't seem to have any kind of cutoff when it comes to sugar. They'll eat it until they get sick.*" Cassian asked about money, how they paid them. "*That's all they want. To be treated well, of course, and not to be yelled at. I never raised my voice to any of them, and to do what I said with the flowers and sugar. They're just happy to be working for dragons.*"

"*I have to give them something.*" He told him that he should ask them. "*I'm sure that they can't take our money and use it, but what of things that I find around the place for them? I read once in a book that they enjoyed colorful glass and beads.*"

"*As I said, I don't know about that, but ask them. Someone will be in charge of the group. And they'll tell you who they are. I've forgotten the name of the little creature that comes to me; I'll have to get better at that. But now that I think about it, I have been known to give them some things that I might find while I'm out. They like bits of cloth they can use. Believe it or not, they like those old-fashioned pop lids, you remember the kind I'm talking about. They use things like that in their homes. But ask. That's the best way to treat them right and have them wanting to help you.*" He'd think of something to do. And Kings was right, asking them would cause no confusion about what they might want. "*Also, you might want to give them a room that they can go to when they have time off. Skye set up one of the rooms with lots of windows in it so they can have the sunlight. I'd forgotten about that.*"

After closing the connection with Kings and the

others, he wondered how they would get into his place without knocking at the door. Almost as soon as that thought entered his head, he heard a small whisper of a sound at the front door. Going to see who it was, he wasn't surprised to find a sole faerie with the biggest smile on her face. He stepped back to allow her entrance, and she came in and told him why she was there.

"I wanted to make sure you're ready for us." He said that he was and showed her the room that would be theirs when they lived with him. "Oh, good. So many windows, too. This will be perfect. If you were to leave a window open a small bit for us to come and go, then we'll not bother you again about where we will be staying. This is perfect."

As soon as he opened the window about an inch or two, they started arriving. Not as a horde as he thought, but a few at a time, and they would thank him as they moved by him. Moving back to the door, he stayed out of their way while they got settled. The first faerie that came to him, her name was Buttercup, said that she would be his go-to faerie and that she would be there for the others to make sure they didn't do anything to upset him.

"I was wondering what I need to do to pay you for your time." She shook her head and told him they were pleased to be able to serve him. "But surely there is something that I can repay you with that would make your lives better for doing the same for me."

"I'll ask around. We do like flowers to eat and sometimes, not often, sugar cubes. Also, a bit of water in a dish wouldn't be remiss either." He said he could do that for them. "Good. If there is anything else, then I'll tell you."

"Thank you." She flittered away only to return a few seconds later. "Is there something wrong? I can fix just about anything."

"I'll be your faerie forever if you wish. When we have some time together, we'll form a connection. That way, you can call for me when you are in trouble. We have a lot of the battle warriors with us, too. Some in each house." He said that he'd like that too. "Good. You're a good man, lord Cassian. I'm happy to be serving you."

When she went to the room, he got down a saucer and put some water in it. He did wonder how they drank it, but didn't let that bother him too much. He had help around the house, and that was going to be perfect for him. As he thought of things that he wanted to do for the pip he now had, he knew he was going to have to come up with some rules. He didn't know what they might be right now, but he was sure that he could figure them out as he went. Having a lot of faeries around would be nice, but it might be too overwhelming as well. That was Kings biggest complaint. There were just too many of them around all the time.

By dinner time, he had two rules for them. They couldn't be in the bathroom if he was in there, and they weren't to bother him while he was in his bedroom if the door was closed. Same with his office. If the door was open, they were more than welcome to come and talk to him. Otherwise, he was simply busy with work and couldn't be bothered while on the phone and such. Also, he noticed that the house was beginning to look different with them all there.

The carpets had been cleaned. He'd been trying to remember to vacuum when he was home, but it was too much effort when he was exhausted after a day of working. He abhorred dusting and never did it unless he was having company. Then he would only dust the room he thought they'd be in. Not only were all the rooms seemingly dust-free, but he could swear that all the windows in the house had been shinier than they'd ever been before.

The house seemed warmer, not in the heated-up sort of way but as if they had made his home homier. He found himself going around the house and finding new things that he'd not noticed before. There were flowers in the main hall. Little touches of light that made the room feel like it was brighter. He loved having the faeries around now, if they were going to give his home the warm touches that he was seeing now.

"Lord Cassian, there is a person at the main gate to the house who wishes to bring you a package. Did you have something coming?" He said that he did, he'd ordered some things online just last night. "There is a brownie at the gatehouse now that will ring the house when you're in attendance. He said that if you could give him a list of people to allow in, he'll only let you know that they're here and not ask you about them."

"I can do that." He got his package in record time. Usually, he would be notified about something being delivered and have to search everywhere for the package. This was so much nicer. Something else that he was going to have to talk to Buttercup about was how he would pay the brownie and whether they would be human-like, too. So many questions popped into his mind at different times of the day. He asked her what his name was. "Just so I can acknowledge them when I see them."

"His name is Henry Fonda. Something that he picked up from a television show that he was watching. He's quite proud of that name, sir." He laughed a little, thinking of the movies that he used to watch with the late actor in them. "Shall I tell him that you're pleased with his work so far? Brownies can be quite the handful when they have nothing to do. Lady Earth thought that he'd work well at your gate for you. She is going to make it so that all the houses have gate houses for some brownies to work in."

"Excellent idea. Yes, I can see where that would come in handy for everyone." He did too. Just so people didn't pull in the driveway to see a dragon all the time. Also, the package delivery system was perfect for them. "I hope that we can all have this special job taken care of."

By evening, he was as happy as he'd ever been about having the faeries in the house. He did realize that he had fewer than Kings had, but he could see the usefulness of having them around. They made him feel less lonely in the house, too, and they did brighten up the rooms they were in. He'd never had such fun trying new things before as he was having the little people at his beck and call. Not that he ordered them around all that much, but he did love being able to talk to them when they came to him with questions.

Chapter 9

Raven loved her job. She'd been working in the fast food restaurant for the past five years since turning sixteen and needing some extra cash for a car that she wanted to purchase. Since then, she'd not just gotten her a second or third-hand car, but she'd been promoted to head cashier, too. It paid a little more than she'd been making, and she got to be the one in charge while they were all busy at the cash register.

But today, sadly, was her last day. She was going to finish her college education and become a lawyer. Taking night classes all this time had suited her needs well, but now that she was having to intern and go to classes, it had become a bit too much for her. She'd been able to secure enough grants to not have to work, but she was going to have to pinch her pennies until they screamed for mercy.

"What are you going to do with all your free time?" So many customers thought that she was just quitting so as not to have to work anymore. "I bet you have a list a mile long to do when you're off." "I'm betting that in a month you'll be back like nothing happened." "You're too good a worker not to have a job." Her favorite one, people said to her, was "So you've won the lottery, have you?" She could only wish that the last one was true.

But the people that she worked with knew what she was doing. Not all of them understood her need for higher education, but she didn't care. It had been a dream of hers to be a lawyer since she'd been to her first court hearing at six years old.

Her parents were divorced. And they both wanted her to live with them. Not because they loved her. No, her parents only wanted the child support the other would have to pay. She knew this the day she was seated in the big chair by the judge and asked what her opinion was about living with one or the other of them. She looked at the older man and told him she didn't want to live with either of them, but would very much like to live with her grannie, who had been raising her since she could walk. That threw a big bomb on the way things went after that.

So at age six, she moved in with her grannie permanently, and both parents had to pay the dreaded child support to her mother's mom. They didn't want her anyway, and with them having to pay support, they didn't feel as if they had to visit her either. Fine by her, she loved her grannie very much.

"It's time for your break." She nodded at the assistant manager and grabbed her drink. She got a free meal daily, but had long since gotten tired of the same food daily and brought herself in something to eat now. As she was eating her PB&J, peanut butter and jelly sandwich, she tried to ignore the man whose office was right next to the breakroom. "You know there's a fat bonus for any one of us who can talk you into staying just where you are. You should think of the people you're leaving behind. They're going to miss you."

"I'm leaving here, not dying. They can visit if they want." The fact was that no one knew where she lived, and she liked that just fine, too. She loved her job and only somewhat liked the people that she worked with. "I'm going to school and I won't have time to work a full-time schedule. Not even a part-time one."

She didn't point out to him either that if she stayed, she wouldn't be leaving anyone behind. Sometimes Daniel didn't think before he spoke, and it made him sound stupid. Or maybe he was. She didn't really care. He kept at her during her break about leaving and the bonus so much that she took the last fifteen minutes of her break outside in the cold.

Her classes started next week, and she was looking forward to studying a bit more. She didn't own a television or even a radio, but she could travel a bit, and she was going to see her grannie and hang out with her for a couple of days. Then she was going to get her apartment in order before everything started happening.

When her break was over, she went back in to clock in and start on the register again. While she'd been gone, they had put someone else on her line, and she decided to clean up the lobby. It was a mess since kids were off school today, and it took her an hour to get things back to looking good. One of the other people she worked with said they'd take out the trash, and she was all for that. It had been cold standing out there, and she was glad that she didn't have to go back out.

At the end of her shift, she was standing to clock out when Daniel started harassing her again. It really was getting old the way he kept at her all the time. She thought because she was older than him, it was what made him think that bossing her around was fun, but she just wanted to do her job and go home. He was making it so that she didn't enjoy coming to work as much with him always on her about something.

"Can you stay over?" She told him no, she already had plans. "Just for an hour. I need someone to watch the lobby for me while I run to the bank. It won't be that bad."

"No. I want to go home. You should have asked me before I made plans and clocked out." He followed her out to her car. "Just leave me alone. As of ten minutes ago, I no longer work here. I want to go home."

"Damn it, why do you have to be such a stubborn bitch all the time about everything? It's just an hour or two. I have to run to the bank, and you can keep an eye on things while I'm gone." She told him that it wasn't her job that he should have gone earlier when there were more people there. "Well, I didn't, did I, and now I'm telling you that you're going to get your ass back in there and wait for me to return. I won't be but a couple of hours, as I have shit I have to do."

"I'm not going back in there." The slap to her face startled her so much that she fell against her car. "What do you think you're doing? You hit me."

"I know what I did, and now you're going to do what I say and get your ass back in there so I can run some errands. I'm sick of you thinking that you're better than anyone else who works here, and now you're going to do what I tell you. I'm your boss." She shook her head, still holding onto her face. When he hit her again, she felt her head hit her car, and the pain was blinding for a second. Just long enough for him to start dragging her by the hair back into the building. This was going too far.

Fighting him to get away from him, she hurt her arm and ribs. The man was tossing her to the cold pavement even as she was trying to catch her breath. He was really hurting her the way he was beating on her, and she knew that she was bleeding from her mouth and nose. There was no telling where else she was bleeding by the time she was inside the building.

"I've called the police." She didn't know who was speaking, but they said that they were recording it too. Daniel didn't seem to mind what they were saying, since she was in the building again, he was leaving. He told her she'd better be there when he returned, too, or he was going to give her worse than he had already. "They're on their way, Raven. I've told them that he's hurting you."

Daniel was going toward the door when he suddenly turned and came back to her. With a punch to her face, she fell backwards and hit the lobby floor. While there, he drew back his leg and kicked her in the ribs. Everything blacked out from that point on.

Waking up, she knew that she was in the emergency room. Moving her body around so that she could see if someone was with her, she cried out in pain. Every part of her body hurt, and she was sure that when she sat up, she was going to be sick too. What had been wrong with him?

"I'm here." She looked in the direction of the voice. "My name is Cassian Savage. I was in the restaurant when you were dragged in."

"He hurt me because he wanted me to stay while he left for a couple of hours." Thinking hurt as well as her jaw, and she asked for something to drink. When she was given a sip of water, she tried to focus on the man in front of her. "I can't make you out. It's like you're a blurry blob."

"Gee, thanks." He laughed, and she decided that he had a good laugh. "Anyway, Daniel was arrested, and your friends turned over the recording of him following you out of the building and to your car. I'm afraid that I arrived too late to stop him from kicking you—you have two broken ribs in addition to other injuries. But he's claiming that since you're his employee, you should have just done what he said, and that wouldn't have had him hurting you. He blamed it all on you."

"Of course he did. He leaves like that every day and is gone for a few hours. No one ever said anything because he usually leaves someone in charge, and it's good to get away from him. Today he decided that I was going to watch things while he was gone. It's my last day, and I'd already clocked out for good." She wondered why she was telling this man what had happened when all she wanted to do was beg someone for something for the pain. "Who are you again?"

"Cassian Savage. You have a concussion as well. This is the third time we've talked. They said you might have a raging headache, too. Did you want me to call someone for something for pain?"

"Yes, please. I'm sure you have better things to do than to wait around here for me to get meds." He said that he was enjoying himself. "Good for you. I don't know if you know this or not, but it's not terribly romantic to enjoy a woman who is in pain right now."

He laughed again. While she was getting something in her IV, the meds just floated over her. He sat down in the chair again and picked up what she thought was a newspaper. Well, if he wanted to just sit around while she napped, good for him.

The police came to see her a few minutes after she got her pain medication. They asked her to tell them what had happened, and she couldn't believe that Cassian or whoever he was didn't leave. They didn't even make him go. After telling them everything she could remember, Cassian told them that he had knocked Daniel out with his fist, and that was where he was when they had arrived. Flat out on the floor was a good place for her former boss.

"Did he ever hit you before?" She said no, but so far as she knew, no one had ever challenged him before. "And what made you do it this time? Was there something that you said to him or he said to you that set him off?"

"Today was my last day, and because I was leaving, he said something about not getting a bonus that was being offered if someone could get me to stay. I didn't know anything about that until my lunch break, where he insisted that my going to college wasn't as important as him getting the bonus that was there for the taking." The officer asked her if she wanted to press charges. "Yes. There wasn't any reason for him to knock me around like he did so that he could go on break for a couple of hours."

"Does he usually take a two-hour break in the afternoon?" She told them that he did on her days working, but she didn't know if he did it on her days off. "Has he ever left you in charge before. Or in this case, wanted you to be in charge before?"

"No. I don't want to be in charge. I was head cashier, but I didn't have to do anything but take over the register when someone had a break." The officers asked her again if he'd left her in charge before. "No. Like I said, I don't want to be in charge."

The hospital was going to keep her overnight because of the head injury. By the time she was settled in her room, her manager and the district manager came into her room. She didn't want to keep going over the same questions all the time, but she knew in order for Daniel to get what he deserved, she was the one with the power to put him there. She never liked him anyway.

All the time she was being questioned, Cassian was right there with her. He even, at one point, said that she'd had enough questions for one day and that they'd have to come back tomorrow. She didn't understand why her bosses left when they did, but was kind of glad for it. She really had had enough of the same questions over and over.

"What happens now, do you know?" Cassian told her that Daniel would stay in jail until such time as the police charged him with something. "I think they have a lot to choose from. Did you hear that he's not supposed to leave the building with one of us in charge? I wonder how they didn't know that."

"It sounded to me like he was doing a lot of things that they didn't know about. Hopefully, they fire him. But probably they'll send him to anger management school and be done with it. Worse things have happened." She thought he might be right about the anger management classes. She'd read that someplace how people who worked for the place that she had were sending their 'family members' to classes rather than waste all the time that they paid for training for them. Yes, she thought, worse things have happened.

"Why are you here?" She still thought that he was somewhat blurry, but didn't say that to him. The nurses had asked if she wanted anything for pain, and when she got it, she realized that the man had been there with her all day. And now it was nearly nine o'clock, and he was still hanging around. "You have to have better things to do than to just sit around a hospital bed all evening."

"What do you know about shifters?" She said that she knows that she works with a couple, but other than that, she didn't know anything. "They mate for life, did you know that much?"

"No. And why would I care? I'm just a plain human who has been hurt. You didn't answer my question." He said that he was her mate and that he belonged to her. "Belong to me? What does that even mean? And I don't want a mate. I have my things and my life just the way I want them to be."

"I'm afraid that it doesn't work that way. I've found you or you've found me, I'm not sure how you want to say that, and you're stuck with me." She rolled to her side and didn't look at him. "We don't have to talk about this now. I know you must be hurting."

"As I said, I have things the way that I like them, and I'm not going to be bossed around by you. You can take your mate business someplace else. I don't want you." He laughed again, and she was beginning to think there was something wrong with him. "Go away. I've had a really shitty day today, and I don't need you and your laughing ass here with me."

"That's very hurtful. And I have no intentions of bossing you around. I know you have a life. While you were out on the floor, one of your coworkers said you were going to college to become a lawyer. I was one of those at one time. I don't remember how long ago — what's the matter?" She turned in the bed to look at him.

"I just realized who you are. You're one of the Savage guys. The cousins or something along those lines. You're supposed to have more money than Midas, as my grannie says." He didn't bother denying it. "I don't need some rich guy trying to make me into his plaything either. I have a life that I like just fine." He laughed. This time, it was as if he'd gotten a really good kick out of her woes. "You're certifiable. Has anyone ever told you that before?"

"My brother, Brenin, said that I do laugh when things around me aren't that funny. But sometimes I get a kick out of what people are saying, so I laugh." She rolled back to her side, careful of her ribs this time. "I think you're beautiful and will fit right in with my family, Raven."

"We'll see." She had to roll to her back; her ribs were hurting her too badly to sleep on her side. "We're not having sex. I draw the line at being your plaything." When he laughed again, she willed herself to sleep. The man was insane if he thought that she'd just come along nicely with him.

~*~

Standing up, he stretched when he knew she was asleep. Cassian thought that having a mate was fun so far. Of course, she was going to be tough to make her believe that he wasn't going to boss her around. Also, she wasn't going to be a plaything either. He thought that was funny that she was so dead set against having him in her life that he caught himself smiling every once in a while just thinking about her.

Daniel was lucky that there had been people around when he'd realized that Raven was his mate. He might well have shifted and killed him right where he stood. He'd been eating in the little fast-food place when he noticed that everyone was standing by the door to the parking lot. There wasn't any way that he could have reacted quicker, as he was shocked to see what the man was doing to the woman. The man was beating her and knocking her to the ground like she was nothing more than a stick.

Walking into the hallway where the nurses were, he nodded to one of them when they asked if everything was all right. The only reason he'd been able to stay was because Kings had pulled a few strings for him in order to get himself a free pass to stay in Raven's room. He couldn't leave her, not injured the way that she was.

Every time he looked at her face, his dragon wanted to find the man responsible and kill him. Not just wound him like he'd done to Raven, but to rip his throat out and stomp on him as his dragon. The doctors said she'd be all right, but it didn't lessen the fact that he'd beaten an innocent woman like he had.

Cassian had met men like Daniel before. Given a little bit of power over someone, it went straight to their heads. Daniel was the kind of man that the police were forever screening for with tests to keep them out of their departments. They would abuse their power and people, too. It was worse that they were able to carry a gun.

Walking the floor, he was careful not to make any

kind of disruption for the nurses. They were all working hard, and he didn't want to get in their way. Going back to the room that Raven was in, he sat down on one of the nice loungers and set it up so that it was leaning back for him. Closing his eyes, he thought about what Raven was going to bring to his life. He could already feel a bit more magic around his body and was happy for that. The need to heal her was paramount, but he held off. People would be questioning everything if she were suddenly healed up from her beating. His body tensed up when he thought of the damage that had been done to her.

She had two broken ribs and several that were badly bruised. Her wrist was broken, and she had several cuts on her face that had needed stitches. There was a long jagged cut on her head where she hit the car, they told him, and that had required seventeen stitches on its own. It was also the point where she'd been concussed as well. Her legs and other arm were cut up, and she had both her eyes blackened, and her nose was bruised. She was, in a word, a mess. And all because some jackass had decided that he had power over her and was going to make her do what he wanted.

Every time he thought of Daniel, he wanted to kill him. Which wasn't helping him sleep. He had a big day tomorrow, and being worked up wasn't going to make it easier on him. Tomorrow, he was going to have to work hard in convincing his new mate that he'd never do her any harm and that she'd be safe with him. He would even make sure that her grannie was all right.

The elderly woman couldn't make it to the hospital until tomorrow. Her driver for the day, a next-door neighbor who took her to appointments and such, was in for the night and didn't drive after dark. He was going to send someone for her first thing in the morning and make sure that she could see her granddaughter before she was released. She'd been ever so grateful that he'd called her.

It was Kaida who had gotten the idea that someone needed to call for her. She'd rumbled through her mind gently and had found that she'd been living with her grannie. Getting the phone number was easy after that. Someone at the police station had known about her grannie and had given him the number to call her. Cassian remembered the conversation well.

"You tell me what time you get up in the morning, and I'll have a car there waiting to bring you in. Then, when you've had enough visiting, I'll get one to send you home in, too. No point in bothering your neighbor when I can easily do this for you." She told him she was up at six in the morning. "How about I have the car there at seven, that way you can have plenty of time to get going and have some breakfast too."

"That sounds about good to me." He told her his name twice, but he wasn't worried about her not remembering it. She was stressed, and he knew it. "She's all I've got in the whole world. Well, I suppose that's not true. I do have my daughter, but she ain't worth nothing. I don't think she's even seen her daughter since I won custody of her all those years ago. Her daddy neither." She snorted as she spoke to him about Raven. "Sorrier bunch of people you'd ever want to know. Not that you'd want them around. They forever had their hands out all the time until they had to start paying me some money to keep my girl. Not that I would have ever charged them, but the courts said they had to, so I got me a check from the two of them every month like clockwork."

She had a terrible laugh. It was like a braying jackass that had been startled from behind. But he'd bet anything that she didn't care. She made no apologies about it and seemed to enjoy laughing about things. It made him smile when she laughed the first time.

"I'll take good care of the two of you, too. You don't have to worry about anything so long as I'm around." And he'd be around forever, too, he wanted to tell her, but didn't. He didn't know her all that well as yet. "She's not going to be able to be alone after she leaves the hospital, so I'll have the two of you stay with me until she's better. All right?"

She said it was fine, but he could hear the confusion in her voice. He'd be that way, too, if some stranger told you that he was going to take you home with your hurt granddaughter. Getting up when Raven stirred around on the bed, he made sure that she wasn't in any pain so that she could rest. Giving her just enough magic that would keep her in a deeper sleep so that she could heal faster.

At midnight, they came in to wake her and ask her some questions. It was protocol for head injuries, and he understood that. He didn't have to like it, but he did understand why they did it. To make sure that the injury wasn't getting any worse.

Just as he was settling back down in the chair, Bluebonnet came to see him. He had been wondering how they were getting along at his home, and she assured him that things were coming along nicely. She was also able to give him his laptop as well as the two books he'd been reading that were by his bedside. Blue smiled at him when he thanked her.

"I will have fresh clothing for you in the morning should you wish it." He said that he would and thanked her again. "Would you like for me to bring you any food? There is plenty at the house that I can make sure you have. It will be no problem should you wish for something from a restaurant either."

"I'm fine right now. I'll get something here for breakfast before Mrs. Lanning shows up. She's Raven's grandmother on her mother's side." Blue told him that she'd been in Raven's mind and she's been able to make the master bedroom to her liking. "That's something that I wouldn't have thought of. If there is anything you need, just let me know, and I can get it for you. She should be fine once she's able to get out of here."

"That's wonderful news, my lord." She asked him about things at the house, and he was able to tell her what was going on. He also told her about the room that she was using for herself and the other faeries. It was a big room, and he didn't mind them setting up a small place for them to have crafts, too. They all made their own furniture. "They are loving the room and the setup. Some of them have been starting on larger homes because of how much room they have. I'm so happy for them."

"I'll need to get a faerie for Raven so that she can have the same benefits that I do. The magic cannot heal her as yet. There are police involved in her getting hurt, and they might not understand if she was suddenly well. But I would like for her to have a connection with someone so that if something ever happens, we can get to her much faster than I was able to today." She asked what had happened, and he told her. "So you can see that she's going to need time to heal on her own and not raise any questions about her injuries. Understand?"

"I do my lord. We don't want her to be questioned about the manner in which she was able to heal. Humans don't understand that at all." There was a great deal that humans didn't understand, but since his mate was one of them, he was fine with that. The less they knew, the better off every shifter would be. Especially those with a closed mind. He'd seen plenty of those in his lifetime, too. People who only saw things that they thought were real. "I shall return to the house now, sire, if there is no more need of me this evening."

After sending her on her way, he sat back and looked at things on his computer. He wasn't really concentrating on anything, so when he saw the article about Raven getting hurt, he was watching the video that accompanied it twice before he realized that it was her.

It was small wonder he didn't do more damage to her human body the way that he was treating her. All that did was get his anger up again, and it took another walk around the floor to get himself to calm down. He was hoping that Daniel would get out of jail. He was going to teach him a few lessons in how to treat a woman. Especially his woman.

Chapter 10

Kings decided that he'd had enough work done for the day. It was only around one o'clock in the afternoon, and he was getting out of his office and going to find something to do other than paperwork and worrying about being king of his kind. There was plenty enough to do without him adding to his workload by trying to figure out what kind of mess he was in because someone had decided that he needed to be in charge. What if he didn't want to be in charge?

He'd been asking himself that same question several times a day for a week now. There were people out there who needed someone to be boss, but he didn't believe or think that he was the solution. They needed to pick someone who cared about the lives of other dragons. He just wasn't it. He saw Brenin walking toward the library when he suddenly found himself downtown.

The whole town wasn't much of a town. There were three stoplights, two gas stations, as well as four pizza shops. Oh, and a McDonalds across the street from the town proper. On Friday night in the fall, nearly all the town came to see the local football team play, and girls' basketball was a big hit in the early spring.

Houses mixed well with the local shops, and he loved the local library because it was a center for adults to hang out with each other while reading over the free newspaper that came out once a week. There were large trees that lined the main drag, cars in some of the yards, as well as lighted decorations on the light poles at Christmas time.

"Where are you headed?" Brenin said the library to return a book, then he was going to get himself a sub for lunch. "Can I join you? I have something that I want to talk to you about. Also, did you hear that your brother found his mate?"

"Sure, I'd be happy for the company. And I heard from him last night. He seems to be enjoying himself. She's a spitfire, he told me." That's what he'd heard, too, and she wanted Cassian to go away all the time. "I'm going over to see them when she gets settled in. Her grannie is living with the two of them as well."

They ordered their lunch and sat down to have it brought to them. Once they had their food and it was set up the way that they liked it, Brenin asked him what he wanted to talk about.

"First, I wanted to say thanks for helping Ace get elected. He is already doing a good job as the mayor. I can see him getting his list done quickly now that he has a place to work from. Did you hear about the votes? Trail only got fifteen votes. That's how many of his family live around here. Though I don't think his wife is very happy. She liked having him working all day." Brenin said thanks about Ace and hadn't heard about the votes. "Yeah, that's sort of sad but good for everyone else."

"I agree with you on Ace getting his list done soon. I saw some of the street workers out taking down the signage from Christmas last year about the parade. I guess we're not having one this year due to budget costs or something like that." They were about finished with their meal when Brenin asked what he wanted to talk about. "I don't have any plans for the rest of the day, so whatever you have going on, we can talk if you want."

"I don't want to be king." He thought that Brenin would laugh at him or tell him it was a done deal. But all he did was ask why it had taken him so long to figure it out. "I don't know, actually. I've been telling myself that I could do a good job of it, but I really can't. I have too many other things going on in my life that I want to do a good job with, too. I have a new mate that I'm still getting to know. There are projects around here that I want to be a part of. And this whole king thing just seems like a stupid job. Did I tell you that I have to go see each region yearly in addition to making sure that laws aren't broken? The laws are broken without me having to travel around the world all the time. Some of them don't even recognize that there can be human mates. If I find one, including my own mate, I'm supposed to destroy them and hope that the dragon gets another mate to come along. That's just barbaric."

"What do you need from me? You know I've got your back." He said he knew that and was glad for it. "You have to tell that Lady Earth person right away. And you know what I was thinking? They went forever thinking that you were being trained without a king. I'm sure they can go a bit longer without one. What are you going to do about the magic?"

He loved talking to Brenin. He just buck shot information at you when something occurred to him.

There wasn't a rhyme or reason behind the way that he asked you things. Just whenever something popped into his head, he would talk to you about it.

"I'm supposed to go and see the Lady Earth tomorrow. I've been studying the books she's given me for weeks now, and I'm no closer to figuring out what I want to do than I was before I started reading them." He half laughed. "These books need to be destroyed and start over. Most of the rules that are in them are too old to deal with now, and the costs for any fines are so little money that it hardly seems worth collecting. Most of them talk about half a percent of whatever cash they have on them at the time of sentencing. I would imagine that most go to their hearings without anything on them, so they don't have to pay. Even though it's probably only about a quarter."

"What are you going to tell her when you see her? I mean, do you have a plan worked out on what you're going to say? What does Skye have to say about this? And if I were you, I'd bring up the fine costs to her. It sounds to me like they'll be paying you more than they're collecting." He said that he's not paid cash but gems. "Oh, good, those are so easy to take to the grocery store and turn in for food. Morons. You probably have a great many gems now. I know that I do. I use them for window dressings. Nobody ever believes that you'd put real diamonds or other gems in your window for the pretty colors."

"I've spoken to Skye and she agrees with me that it's a stupid job to have. Especially one that has so many rules that I have to follow. Like the travel thing too. She said that with having to visit each district, there will be no time for us to have a vacation of our own. Yeah, she doesn't like it either." He asked him again what he wanted from him. "Someone to tell me that it's a stupid job and that I'd be better off quitting it now than before I kill someone when I've had enough."

"That might get you out of the job faster if you were to do that." Again, they both laughed. It felt good to have made the decision now that he had, and he relaxed a bit. "I wouldn't take it even if they offered me money instead of gems. All the rules aside, like you just said, you've only just found your mate, and you want to get to know her better. I'm thinking that alone would have me not taking it."

"I'm going to tell her in the morning. Skye doesn't have to go with me, but I'm going to see if she'll go to tell her that she doesn't want the job either." Brenin finished off his dinner and asked for another soda. He loved the clear kind of drinks. He said that they gave him a clean taste in his mouth. "Thanks for listening to me. You don't know how much I appreciate you just being here for me."

"Now that Cassian has his mate, I'm thinking that the rest of us will be getting ours, too. I might need you for advice when she comes along." Kings said that he'd be better off talking to the mates rather than the men because they could tell him what not to do. "I can see that too. They'd be able to keep my head out of my ass with my mate too, I'm thinking."

They talked a bit more about how they were going to the first football game of the season. Also, about how they'd be around when the first trick-or-treaters came to their house. That was all on Brenin. His way of just casual talking was like listening to a round about speaker. He'd get to the point sooner rather than later.

Walking back home, he found Skye in the kitchen with Trevor. He told her what decision he'd come to and asked her if she'd go with him tomorrow. After she said she would tell her, at the same time, she didn't want to be queen, they'd celebrate by having a cookout with steaks. He was fine with that.

"I have my test in my outdoor classes on Saturday. They were going to have them from Friday to Sunday, but they forgot about the football game going on Friday night. Are you guys going?" Both he and Skye said they wouldn't miss it and were happy that he was going as well. "I can't wait to see them play. Some of the pack are on the team, too. I've made some pretty good friends at the pack house and the high school as well. There are a lot of nice people in both places."

"I'm glad that you're having such a good year, Trevor. To think you didn't think you'd like high school when you first moved here." He said he'd learned to give things a chance. "Good for you. It's like this king job. I gave it my best, and I realized that it wasn't for me. I don't want to be in charge of such a large area of dragons when they've been governing themselves for so long. Hopefully, she's all right with us stepping down."

"She'll just have to be. I'm at my wits' end trying to make sense of those books she gave us. And even if she'd have given us different books that made more sense than the ones we have, I still wouldn't want to take on this job. There are just too many things that they expect of us, which means we don't have a life." Kings said that was the perfect answer. They'd have no life if they took the job. "Besides that, no one asked us if we wanted to be king or queen. They just gave us a bunch of power that hurt like hell and assumed we'd be all right with it. No way in hell would I have said yes if asked. And especially now that we've had a chance to look it over, I'd say no again."

Supper was just sandwiches. The cook was off today and tomorrow to go and visit her children, and they were going to have whatever they could forage out of the freezer and cabinets. He supposed that they could have ordered out, but that was just too much effort for what they were doing. Tomorrow was going to be a big day in talking with Lady Earth, and he wondered about a few things.

Would she take back the magic that she'd given them? He didn't mind. It would be one less thing that he'd have to mess with. Kings laughed a little and thought that he was getting lazier in his old age. But if she did take the magic away, he wondered if it would hurt as badly as it had when she gave it to them.

Then there were the faeries. He'd gotten used to having them around since he'd shared with his family. He didn't care if she took them back, but it would be a huge disappointment for him if she did. They were turning out to be quite helpful around the house, and he was going to miss them. Then there had been the perks of going to the other world to visit the Lady.

The realm was otherworldly and beautiful. The air smelled so much cleaner and fresher while there, and sometimes he would linger a little longer just to be in it. The colors seemed to be brighter as well, especially in the trees and flowers.

"Have you given any thought as to what you're going to say to her?" Supper was over, and it looked to him like they were going to bed early as well. "I'm going to flat-out tell her that I don't want the job. I know that I'm going to have to have good reasons, but I frankly don't care if I have any. I didn't ask for the job in the first place."

"I've been thinking about what I was going to say to her for the last week. It's basically the same as what you're saying. We didn't ask for it. Not to mention all the things that we're going to have to give up if we were to take it, like getting to know one another without traveling all over the world several times. I told Brenin about how we were going to get paid, and he made a joke about how that's easy to change out for food. He's a great guy to have around when you have a hard decision to make, don't you think?" She told him that she'd been complaining to Kaida, who agreed with her. "Yes, I can see her being a big advocate about not being asked to do the job."

"If I wanted a full-time job, I'd find something that I'd like to do and be able to learn it in a reasonable amount of time." She sat down on the couch where he was sitting. "What do you think she'll do? That's my biggest worry. That she'll kill us off because we told her no. I mean, she did say that she created all dragons, didn't she?"

"I'm hoping she won't do that. It would be scary to think that just because we tell her no, that we don't want the job, that she'll just destroy me. I'd bargain with her about your life, however. I'd want you to be turned back into a human and allowed to live." She said she couldn't go on without him. "Oh, Skye, I know I wouldn't be able to live without you either."

As they made their way up to the bedroom after leaving the living room, he made sure that the house was securely locked up for the night. It was getting colder out, and he didn't want the least bit of coldness to come in either. As he was going up the stairs, he realized just how tired he was.

He'd not been sleeping well, worrying about this king job, and he thought that tonight, with his decision made, he'd sleep very well. He thought that he should be worrying about what she was going to do to them, but he just didn't care at this point. Kings was dragging by the time he had stripped down and gotten into bed. Almost as soon as he snuggled up with Skye and closed his eyes, he was sound asleep.

~*~

Listening to them talk about the job as king and queen, Lady Earth couldn't find fault with what they were saying. She'd ambushed them into taking the job, and since she'd made it clear that she had created dragons, they'd just simply be too afraid to not take the job when she'd gone to so much trouble in making them take it.

"We want to have a life. With this job, we'd have nothing." She didn't bother answering them when they said things like that—They'd said it several times now that they'd have no quality of life taking the job. What did they think she had with her job? No, best not to bring up how much she hated her own job to them. "So what are you going to do?"

She realized that she might well have missed something. They were both looking at her like they were expecting an answer to a question she didn't listen to. Instead of admitting that she didn't know what they had said, she instead asked what they thought that she should do.

"First and foremost, I don't want you to kill either of us." She must have really missed something important if they'd gotten that far in the conversation. "You can take back the magic if you wish, but we like the faeries. But you can take them back, too, since we're not going to be doing the job."

"No one likes the job that they do." She thought about it for about a second before she admitted to them that she didn't like hers either. "So you see, I didn't think beyond the need and I didn't want to have to mess with it anymore so I gave it to you. All this time, I assumed that you'd be training and doing the job so that I didn't have to bother with the dragons. I so love those creatures, but I have so many other things that pull me in all kinds of directions all the time."

"Maybe you need some help with your job." She nodded at Skye and told her that there was no one who could do her job as well as she could. "Perhaps not everything, but I'm betting that there are people who can take over portions of your job. Say, watching over the faeries. They seem to be a handful unless they're busy. And too many of them in one place."

"How did you fix that? If I remember, a great many of them were sent to your home." Kingston told her what he'd done. "That's a splendid idea. And it worked? They're no longer pestering you all the time for things to do? You know, there are only so many flowers that they can take care of. Perhaps I should send them around in your realm for things to do."

"There are plenty of flowers they can be caring for over there, yeah, sure." They looked at each other, and she wanted to ask them what was going on. "What's up with you? You seem really distracted today."

"I have so much to do. I was hoping that you'd take over the dragons so that I don't have to mess with them anymore. I mean, since I thought you were messing with them for me, I never heard from them, so perhaps they've been taking care of themselves. I don't know. I'm overwhelmed and overworked right now." She felt the tears fill her eyes. "I'm sorry. I'm this all-powerful person, and I'm whining like I'm a toddler without their nap."

"Is there anything we can do to help you that doesn't involve us taking over the dragons?" She laughed. It had startled her; it had been so long since she'd had an occasion to laugh about something. And she realized that she'd missed it. "What do you do for your organizational skills. I mean, do you have a daily plan that you follow? That's the only way I get anything done is to have a set plan on what I'm doing."

"I don't have time to plan out a plan for anything. Even in the spring, when we're our busiest, do I have a plan about how to plant things. I think I messed up last spring in forgetting to plant a couple of fields, and that's why the faeries are without anything to do this fall. I've just messed up so many things that I'm behind in everything." A large map of her realm appeared in the room, and she looked at it as other things began to appear. Colored pencils, rulers, and markers. There were even sticky notes that she so loved to use when she had time to make notes. "This is all very lovely, but I have all this in my office."

"But you're not using them." The map was placed on the table with all the other things around it. "While I don't have any idea where things are planted, I can assume that it's someplace on this map."

For an hour, she worked on the map with the two of them. It came to her that she had missed three fields of flowers being planted, and that was why everyone was just sitting around. After they deemed the map filled out, she looked it over.

"This is lovely." The fields were marked off, and there was a flower drawn in different areas around the map. With the dates too that she should be planting things, she was well on her way to having all the fields planted by May. A good month to start having plants bloom. The more she looked at the map, the more information she could see on it.

There were sticky notes on what should be planted in each field. And if she did it correctly, then some of the fields could be planted twice. She could see herself getting ahead of the game. But before she told them that she still had other things that needed her attention, Skye called the faeries in that were forever around the castle she lived in and spoke to them.

"This is the map of flowers. You'll follow these dates with the other planters and have all the fields planted by May. There is no need for you to be behind, as it's all laid out for you to work with." They nodded and took the map away. Then she looked at her. "One less thing you have to worry about now. What else do you have to organize?"

For the next several hours, they made up maps of things that had to be done. Then, like the first time, the map was sent with a group of faeries to get started on. Even the fields that hadn't been planted this year were being worked up so that the soil was ready for the seeds in the spring planting. Group after group of faeries were assigned work schedules to get done, and she couldn't believe how much they were getting finished up in a day.

"I used to be organized at one time. But I forgot to keep at it. Then, after a while, it got to be too much to go back to it." Skye told her that now that the faeries were busy, she could concentrate on other things that needed her attention." I'd forgotten what it's like to have nothing that is pounding me in the head all the time. It's a wonderful feeling knowing that I have the faeries busy and I'm able to work on something more. Thank you so much. I just can't thank you enough for this."

For the first time in what seemed like forever, she had a few minutes of time on her hands. Not only were the others busy doing their work, but there didn't seem to be a cloud hanging over her either. This was just what she needed: someone to come in and make her set things right.

When she was ready for bed after the couple left — she'd repaid them by giving them more magic that they didn't know about, and she'd given them access to her realm when they wanted. She loved the fact that they were still leery of her and what she'd do to them after the dragon debacle.

Lady Earth did ask them to write up rules that would be more suitable for this time in a dragon's life. There were so few of them left that she wanted to make sure that they were around for a long time yet to come. She wanted to have rules that they'd gladly follow and wouldn't be taxed too much in the way of fines, so that they'd not be without either. There was a lot to learn about dragons, she discovered. And every day, she was going to find something positive about herself, too.

The next morning, when she got up, there were no faeries in line to talk to her. They were working the fields and doing their jobs in a way that things would be ready when the first seed was to be planted in the early spring. There was time for a cup of tea, time for her to look over her schedule for meetings, and even enough time that she was able to smell the new blooms that were coming up in the glen.

By noon, she was still not overwhelmed. Every creature was working at something, and she wasn't being hounded by anyone. It was a glorious way to start her day. After her noonday meal, she was ready to tackle the list of jobs that she'd been putting off for a while now and get them organized so that she wasn't behind with them.

At the end of the fifth day, she was no longer stressed out, nor was she overwhelmed. Things were getting done in a timely manner, and she was able to fit in a few minutes every day for herself. And she owed it all to her dragons.

She wanted to find a fitting gift for them and thought about it for the next several days. There was always more magic that she could give them, but that wouldn't be something that she'd want either. They had told her that it was enough to mess with now.

"Mistress?" She turned to look at Charlene, one of

her most prized friends and a faerie. "We have found a pip of brownies that have been left to their own devices last fall. I was thinking that we could send them to the other world and put them in places that would benefit other creatures in places like the courthouses and hospitals. We've been told that there is magic for them to have. If you would agree, then I can get them set up there and we'd have a worker to help all shifters."

"Excellent idea. I love that. We can let the dragons know who it is so they know who to call on when needed." Charlene said that she'd take care of it right away. "Tell me something. I'd like to repay them for their kindness last week. What do you think they'd like in the way of a gift from me?"

Charlene smiled and said she knew exactly what to give them. When told, Lady Earth thought it the perfect gift to give them and knew just how she was going to present it to them when the time was right. Oh yes, she thought this was going to be epic for all of them and in the future for her special dragons.

Time seemed to be marching on for her, and she was getting so much more done. Thanks wholly to the dragons that she dearly loved. She was glad now that they weren't going to be king and queen. She had so many other uses for them that her mind was buzzing with ideas.

For the first month, she had to continually check her schedule to make sure that she was on the right path. And while not giving up on the thing, she did make adjustments to her schedule to get even more things accomplished. Her days were brighter and more productive than they'd ever been before. Even when she made out her own schedule and followed it, she'd never gotten this much done.

Denise, another of her favorite faeries, was taking on jobs and making sure that things were just the way they needed to be in the realm. She was happy with her making decisions about everyday things that didn't need her approval. Doing a great job, she was going to have to think of a perfect gift for her as well as Charlene. Given time, she knew she'd have to give all her workers the perfect gifts; just thinking about what they'd be would be hard. But it would come to her sooner or later.

There was no reason for her to sleep, but she did have time now to take a power nap, something humans did a couple of times a week. It would get her through the most difficult of days and make them seem so much easier to deal with. There was time now for the simplest of things to get done, and she would be forever grateful to the couple who helped her for the rest of her days.

Before You Go...

HELP AN AUTHOR

write a review

THANK YOU!

Share your voice and help guide other readers to these wonderful books. Even if it's only a line or two your reviews help readers discover the author's books so they can continue creating stories that you'll love. Login to your favorite retailer and leave a review. Thank you.

AWARD WINNING, BESTSELLING AUTHOR

Kathi S. Barton is an award-winning and bestselling author known for her steamy paranormal romances and unforgettable characters. A recipient of the prestigious Pinnacle Book Achievement Award, her books have topped the charts on Amazon and All Romance eBooks, earning her a loyal global readership.

Kathi lives in Nashport, Ohio, with her husband, Paul. When she's not crafting passionate love stories set in magical worlds, she enjoys camping, exploring local auctions, and attending county fairs, where Paul showcases his artwork and pottery. Her creative spark—fueled by a muse she describes as a cross between Jimmy Stewart and Hugh Jackman—brings her stories to vivid, heartfelt life.

Paranormal romance with plenty of heat is her favorite genre, and she loves connecting with her readers. Feel free to reach out—Kathi would love to hear from you.

Email: aaronskiss@gmail.com
Blog: kathisbartonauthor.blogspot.com